Another Waif and Stray

'Don't look like that, Ellie! It will be fun having him around. Besides, Jakey will love him!'

Maddie's expression belied her words. She was pretty easy to read, and it was already clear she was having doubts. No wonder. I stared at the Boxer dog, whose broad chest tensed as it strained on the lead, practically foaming at the mouth in its eagerness to investigate this strange new world.

'Where the hell did you get it? And more to the point, why?'

Maddie had never struck me as a dog lover before. My aunt Joan — Maddie's mum — was far too house proud to allow pets into her home. I'd always thought it a miracle that she'd allowed Maddie to roam free, and not kept her in a kennel. There was no way Maddie would ever have been able to keep a dog as a child, even if she'd wanted one, and as far as I could remember, she'd never shown the slightest interest in doing so. What the heck had possessed her to bring a dog into an already crowded house?

Maddie sighed and collapsed onto the sofa — the pristine, cream, almost brand-new sofa. I wondered how long it would look as immaculate as it did at that moment. Not long, I reckoned, looking at the Boxer dog's shiny red coat. I'd have bet my last fiver that both the sofa and our clothes would be coated in dog hair before long. And how would Maddie react to that? With a massive meltdown, no doubt.

'They didn't want him! Can you believe it? Poor little thing.'

Poor *little* thing! I eyed the broad skull of the dog dubiously. Little wasn't a word I'd have used to describe him. All right, he wasn't of St Bernard proportions, but he was heavyset, and certainly no lap dog. He stared back, big brown eyes looking mournfully at me out of his chestnut face. He had a white chest, and white lower legs, which made him look as if he was wearing two pairs of socks, but the rest of him was a gorgeous shade of reddish brown. I had to admit he was a handsome chap, in a battered, prize-fighter sort of way.

'Who didn't want him?' I asked.

'The owners. Well, there was this card you see, in the shop window. He was being offered for free to a good home. I wasn't going to enquire at first, because I was sure there'd be plenty of people who would want him, but then I got talking to Mrs Wilson who runs the shop, and she told me all about it, and it was so *sad*.'

'Ah.' I nodded, understanding the situation clearly

About the author

Sharon Booth writes about the lighter side of life, love, magic, and mystery. Her characters may be flawed, but whether they're casting a spell, solving a mystery, or dealing with the ups and downs of family life or romance, they do it with kindness and humour.

Sharon is a member of the Society of Authors and the Romantic Novelists' Association, and an Authorpreneur member of the Alliance of Independent Authors. She has been a KDP All-Star Author on several occasions.

She likes reading, researching her family tree, and watching Doctor Who, and Cary Grant movies. She loves horses and hares and enjoys nothing more than strolling around harbours and old buildings. Take her to a castle, an abbey, or a stately home and she'll be happy for hours. She admits to being shamefully prone to crushes on fictional heroes.

Her stories of love, community, family, and friendship are set in pretty villages and quirky market towns, by the sea or in the countryside, and a happy ending is guaranteed.

If you love heroes and heroines who do the best they can no matter what sort of challenges they face, beautiful locations, and warm, feelgood stories, you'll love Sharon's books.

To find out more visit her website:

www.sharonbooth.com

where you can also sign up for her newsletter.

Books by Sharon Booth

There Must Be an Angel
A Kiss from a Rose
Once Upon a Long Ago
The Whole of the Moon

Summer Secrets at Wildflower Farm
Summer Wedding at Wildflower Farm

Resisting Mr Rochester
Saving Mr Scrooge

Baxter's Christmas Wish
The Other Side of Christmas
Christmas with Cary

New Doctor at Chestnut House
Christmas at the Country Practice
Fresh Starts at Folly Farm
A Merry Bramblewick Christmas
Summer at the Country Practice
Christmas at Cuckoo Nest Cottage

Belle, Book and Candle
My Favourite Witch
To Catch a Witch
Will of the Witch

How the Other Half Lives: Part One: At Home
How the Other Half Lives: Part Two: On Holiday
How the Other Half Lives: Part Three: At Christmas

Winter Wishes at The White Hart Inn

Baxter's Christmas Wish

SHARON BOOTH

ISBN: 9798362007201

For Leah and George

at last. The dog was another of my cousin's lost causes. She couldn't resist a sob story and would always step in to help if she could.

To be fair, I could hardly complain, given that I was one of Maddie's lost causes myself, and where would Jake and I have been, if not for her kind heart?

The trouble was Maddie tended to jump in, letting her emotions rule her common sense, but quickly lost interest. I'd had an uncomfortable feeling for a while that time was already running out for us. Maddie hadn't said anything outright, but there had been a distinct change in her attitude lately; a lot of mutterings about Jake's toys, and how much the washing machine was getting used. I had a sinking feeling that a dog only would add to Maddie's stress.

'So, what did Mrs Wilson tell you about him?'

'The owner doesn't want him anymore because his new girlfriend doesn't like dogs. Can you believe it? They've been together for five years, ever since he was a puppy — that's the owner and the dog, I mean, not the owner and the girlfriend. They've probably only been together for five minutes. How shallow can you be? And poor Baxter here is out on his ear because of some stupid woman, who's more than likely afraid of getting dog hairs on her best dress.'

Her lip curled in scorn, and I tried to hide a smile, wondering how Maddie would react when her own clothes were covered in short red hairs. Even so, I felt a sudden pang of sympathy for Baxter and reached out a hand to stroke his silky ears.

He immediately bounded forward, almost pulling Maddie off the sofa and forcing her to drop the lead. Free from all restraint, he hurled himself at me, planted his paws on my shoulders, and gave me a huge slobbery kiss.

'Ugh, get down!' I wiped my face, my nose wrinkling in disgust.

Baxter licked me again, and I tried to push him away, but it was like trying to move a concrete block. He nuzzled into my neck and, hearing him snuffling against my ear, I tried to quell my sudden panic. He was so heavy. He would knock Jake over with no trouble at all.

'What if he's not safe? You don't know anything about him,' I whispered, wondering, as I did so, why I didn't want Baxter to hear. It wasn't as if he would understand was it?

To my relief, Baxter released me and decided to wander round the living room, investigating the premises. As we watched him sniffing every inch of the carpet, I repeated my worries. Jake was only six years old, and no match for a dog of that size if it decided it wanted to play rough.

'Oh, no! Mrs Wilson's known Baxter for ages, and she said he's an angel with children, and so good-natured and affectionate. More than can be said for the owner's girlfriend. I took one look at her and decided he's better off out of it. She couldn't wait to be rid of him.'

'Didn't the owner seem sad to lose him?'

'He wasn't even there. Obviously couldn't be bothered to say goodbye. Poor boy.'

I watched as Baxter stuck his head in the giant plant pot and sniffed the yucca plant that was Maddie's pride and joy. I couldn't help sympathising with him. I knew only too well what it felt like to be dumped for a new model. Luscious Laura was only twenty-two — a full eight years younger than me. Not that I'd counted or anything, and not that it mattered. Age was just a number I reminded myself. Again.

I wondered what Liam was doing now. Did he ever think about me? Did he regret what he'd done? Or was he still so bewitched by his new girlfriend that his wife never even crossed his mind? Ex-wife, I reminded myself, my nails digging into my palms. The divorce had been finalised after all. No going back.

'Get off my yucca!' Maddie jumped up and pulled a reluctant Baxter away, just as he'd stamped one foot in the plant pot.

'I hope he's house trained,' I said. 'That plant would make a great substitute for a lamppost.'

'Oh, no! You don't think he would?'

Looking appalled, Maddie cast a nervous glance around her immaculate living room.

I grinned. 'You said he was five years old, so I expect he's thoroughly house-trained. I was only winding you up.'

Maddie didn't look too sure.

'So, where's his bed? His toys? Has she sent any food for him?'

Maddie shook her head. 'She said his bed was old and shabby and she'd thrown it away, and I don't think it even occurred to her to send his toys. She was obviously a neat freak. You know the type — blonde, glamorous, all made up. A real princess.'

I did my best to hide a smile as my blonde, glamorous, immaculately made-up cousin rambled on.

'Think she thought she was Grace Kelly or something. She was wearing long gloves in the house! Like she was about to go out to some premiere. And she looked at poor Baxter as if he was the filthiest creature on the planet. Bet she's the type who stops halfway through sex to reapply her mascara.' She shook her head in disgust. 'I did get a bag of food for him though. Well, half a bag. Although, come to think of it, she didn't give me any dishes for him…'

Baxter gave a huge sigh and flopped onto the floor. Already, there was a sprinkling of chestnut hairs on the carpet.

'You'll have to get him a bed, and dishes. And some toys. Poor thing, not even a reminder from home to help him settle. Some people have no compassion.'

'Will you watch him for me while I nip out to the pet shop? I won't be long.'

'I can't. I have to collect Jake from school.'

She beamed at me. 'No worries. I'll collect him

while I'm out and about.'

'But the school's in the opposite direction to the pet shop.'

'I'll take the car. I'll have plenty of time. Thanks a lot.'

There was no use arguing, and anyway I didn't feel able to. I owed Maddie, big time. When Liam had broken the news that he'd fallen in love with Laura, it had left me high and dry.

Having decided that the only way we could afford to save for a decent deposit on a house of our own was to stop renting, Liam had approached his mother eighteen months previously to ask if we could all stay at her house for a year or so, while we saved.

It had been a good plan, from his point of view, although from mine it had been a nightmare come to life. His mother had never approved of me, believing I was unworthy of her precious son, so I'd known it was going to be uncomfortable living with her to say the least. Liam had assured me it would be worth it, and as usual I'd gone along with his plans — only to find myself in an impossible situation when he fell for Luscious Laura.

When Liam had moved in with his new love, I'd been desperate to get away from the mother-in-law, who clearly believed that I'd brought the whole catastrophe upon myself.

It had proved impossible for me to find somewhere decent and affordable, and it turned out that Liam hadn't been saving for a deposit for quite some time. Not since he'd fallen for the obvious charms of his bit of stuff who, it seemed, had expensive tastes.

If Maddie hadn't offered Jake and me a home, I dreaded to think where we'd have ended up. And the most devastating thing about it was that Liam didn't appear to care a jot, airily telling me that I'd be fine at his mother's, and it would all sort itself out one way or another. Yeah, right!

As the front door slammed, Baxter lifted his head and looked hopefully towards the hallway.

'Sorry, boy. That was just Maddie going out to get you some new things. Were you hoping to see your master?'

Baxter hauled himself up and padded over to me. He plonked his heavy head on my lap and gave another big sigh. Despite my misgivings, I felt a surge of compassion for the poor dog. I stroked his head between his ears and made soothing noises, while he stood, silent and still, probably wondering where on earth he was and what was happening.

'I know how you feel, Baxter,' I whispered, my eyes pricking with sudden tears. 'It's not easy being cast aside by someone you love is it? At least you have us now, and you have a good home.'

As for Jake and me... I had no idea what was to become of us. I had an uneasy feeling that we'd soon be leaving Maddie's house behind us, and where we'd end up, I dreaded to think.

***

As predicted, Jake was thrilled to meet Baxter. I watched, my heart in my mouth, as Baxter bounced over to greet my son as he arrived home from school, his face flushed with excitement.

'Maddie says we've got a—'

His words were cut off as Baxter leapt through the hallway door and skidded to a halt at his feet.

'Oh, wow! Isn't he gorgeous? Hello, boy. I'm Jake. Who are you?'

'This is Baxter,' I said, noting with relief that Baxter was being very careful around Jake, although he was obviously delighted to meet him. It appeared Mrs Wilson had been right. He knew how to treat small children. One less thing to worry about anyway.

Jake fell to his knees, wrapping his arms around the dog's chest. Baxter emitted some very loud snuffly noises as he sniffed my son's hair, neck, face, and school jumper. I winced, wondering how much drool would be in Jake's hair once the dog had finished his investigations. Whatever Baxter discovered about my little boy from this thorough search obviously pleased him, as he rewarded Jake with a huge lick across his cheek.

Jake giggled, while I felt a teensy bit nauseated as I remembered the horror stories I'd read about all the diseases you could get from allowing a dog to lick your face. Ugh!

'Okay, Jakey. That's enough for now. You'd better get changed, or you're going to be covered in…' I sighed. Too late.

As Jake stood up, his bright blue school jumper was dotted with red hairs. I'd have to put the washing machine on again. His grey trousers were just as bad. What a nightmare.

'Where's Maddie?' I asked.

'Getting Baxter's things from the boot. She's got him loads of stuff, Mum. Is he really going to be living with us forever?'

I swallowed down the lump in my throat. 'Well, he's Maddie's dog now, Jakey. Don't forget, we'll be moving out soon. We can't stay here much longer. It's not fair on Maddie is it?'

'Maddie doesn't mind! Maddie, you don't mind, do you?'

Maddie pushed her way through the front door, staggering under the weight of a huge plastic dog bed, which was packed with carrier bags full of pet shop purchases.

'Can you close the door for me, someone? Oh, my back's killing me. This stuff weighs a ton. Mind what, Jakey?'

'It doesn't matter,' I said hastily, shutting the front door before removing some of the bags from the dog bed. 'Jake, take Baxter back into the living room then go upstairs and change. I'll have to wash your uniform for tomorrow.'

'You wouldn't mind if me and Mum stayed here with you, would you? Mum says we have to move out, but it's nice here, and now you've got Baxter it will be even more fun.'

I daren't look at Maddie and headed straight to the kitchen instead.

Behind me, I heard Maddie muttering, 'Well, the thing is, Jakey, your mum needs her own place. Wouldn't you like it to be just you and her? Your own things around you again? Your own home?'

'Not really a home without Dad though is it?' he answered, and I dropped the carrier bags onto the worktop, feeling sick. 'He won't come back will he? It wouldn't be the same.'

I closed my eyes, trying desperately to hold back the tears. There it was again, that fierce stab of guilt. Why was I the one feeling guilty when it was Liam who'd lied and cheated? Liam who'd walked away and left us behind with hardly, it seemed, a second thought. I'd wondered so often over the last few months if I'd ever really known him at all. Had the young man I'd married nine years earlier really been the sort of person who'd be capable of such cruel disregard for his wife and child?

Yet, as I thought back over our relationship, I had to acknowledge that the signs had been there from the very beginning. Everything had been the way he wanted it: when and where we were married; where we

17

lived; when we started a family; the fact that there was only ever going to be one child…

I wondered, not for the first time, why I'd gone along with his wishes so easily. What had happened to me? How had he managed to chip away at my self-esteem so easily? Why had I accepted life on his terms? Well, to hell with him. He'd done me a favour, moving in with Laura. I had the chance to start doing the things that I wanted to do at last. The question was, what exactly did I want?

The answer came to me with sickening clarity. A decent home for me and Jake, more children, someone who loved me unconditionally. Someone who would never lie, or cheat. Someone who would love Jake as his own. That was my dream. Fat chance that it would ever be my reality.

I gave myself a mental shake and began to unpack the bags, as Maddie dumped the dog bed on the kitchen table. There was no point even thinking such things. The future was Jake and, somehow, I had to find a decent home for him. The problem was, how? I'd asked for more hours at work, but they were fully staffed, and I'd applied for so many full-time jobs I'd lost count.

On my wages from the supermarket the best I'd be able to afford was some dingy flat somewhere in town. It didn't bear thinking about. What kind of life would that be for my precious son?

'I had no idea dogs needed so much stuff!' Maddie

reached over and picked up a carrier bag, rummaging around inside it. 'Look at this. Dog toothpaste and a dog toothbrush. Who knew? How the heck am I supposed to clean his teeth?'

'Rather you than me,' I said. 'I think they've sold you half the shop.'

'He said they were just the basics but, to be honest, I'm not so sure. This lead cost me a fortune.'

'But he already has a lead!'

'I know. But when I described it to the man in the shop, he said it was the wrong sort of lead and sold me this one instead.'

She looked quite puzzled, and despite my worries, I couldn't help laughing. 'He saw you coming. I should have gone with you. I'd have stuck to the essentials.'

'And since when were you so assertive?' demanded Maddie. 'What happened to the girl who wouldn't say boo to a goose?'

'She grew up.' I sighed. 'She had to, pretty fast.'

Maddie put her arm around me. 'I'll make us a cup of tea, then we'll sort all this stuff out properly. Did you say you were washing Jake's school uniform?'

'Yes, sorry. Dog hair. I've bought some washing powder.'

'It's okay, but while you're washing his stuff, you couldn't shove this top in with it, could you? I look like the Yeti with all this hair on me.'

I gave her a wry look. 'Looks like we're going to be doing quite a lot of washing and vacuuming, now you've got Baxter.'

'I know.' Maddie looked pensive for a moment then brightened. 'But he's so lovely, isn't he? He deserves a second chance. It will all be worth it in the end.'

I headed back into the living room to coax Jake away from Baxter and persuade him to change his clothes, but not before I'd noticed Maddie cross her fingers. I had a feeling that my cousin was already wondering what she'd let herself in for, and she wasn't the only one.

Chapter 2
In the Doghouse

'I'm going to kill that dog!' Maddie's face was purple with rage as she waved her handbag in the air. 'Look what he's done now!'

'What's wrong?' I paused in my dusting, noticing that Baxter looked very guilty as he lurked in a corner of the room.

'What do you think's wrong? Look at my bag! He's chewed through the handles. My Prada bag, ruined!'

'Wasn't genuine Prada was it?' Wayne, Maddie's boyfriend, managed to drag his eyes away from the football match on the television long enough to utter an opinion. 'Stop winding yourself up.'

'It may not have been genuine, but it still cost me over a hundred pounds. That wretched dog is driving me insane. Look at his face! He knows he's done wrong, but it won't stop him doing it again will it?'

'I said you were crazy to get a dog. What did you want one for anyway? They're nothing but trouble. You and your lost causes. You're too soft by half, and you always end up regretting it,' Wayne said, casting a sly look at me.

I turned away, refusing to give him the satisfaction of seeing how much his words stung.

Since he'd been on the scene, Maddie had made it even more obvious that she'd like to have her house back to herself. Jake and I were in the way, there was no doubt about it.

There was only one thing for it. I'd have to throw myself on Liam's mercy. The very idea made me want to hurl, but I was only just managing to pay the rent and my share of the bills and food to Maddie. There was barely anything left over to save, and my deposit fund was still pitiful. Liam must have put some money away, surely? He earned plenty as a taxi driver, although, being self-employed, he'd managed to convince the faceless bureaucrats, who knew about such things, that he was barely covering expenses, and had been allowed to pay a nominal sum in child support. It was sickening. Maybe I could threaten to expose him? Blackmail was an ugly word, but so was slum, and I'd no intention of subjecting Jake to a life in some rundown flat somewhere, thank you very much.

'Baxter's probably just bored,' I said. 'Have you been taking him for regular walks?'

Maddie plonked herself down beside Wayne and folded her arms. 'Yes, of course I have. He's just naturally naughty. I'm beginning to see why they wanted rid of him now. Bet it had nothing to do with the girlfriend. I think I've been had.'

'What do you expect when he was free to a good home?' demanded Wayne. 'Always dodgy that. Look at him. He's a pedigree Boxer dog. They're worth good money. Why would they give him away when they could sell him? Had to be something wrong with him, and there's your answer. He's unmanageable.'

'Unmanageable?' I laughed, and began dusting the television, just to annoy Wayne. 'He's hardly that. He's good, most of the time. It's like I said. He's probably bored.'

'Do you mind? United have a penalty! Go and dust somewhere else.'

'It's all right for you, Ellie,' said Maddie. 'You don't have expensive things, but Baxter's destroyed my best shoes, and that pink cashmere jumper that I loved, as well as my bag. He's becoming a liability.'

Wayne grunted. 'You ought to get rid. Anything that's a liability should go. I've been telling you that for ages.' He glared at me, leaving me in no doubt as to whom he was referring, and I marched into the kitchen, slamming the door behind me.

For a moment I leaned against the sink, my heart pounding as I tried to quell the rage, then I put the polish and duster away and headed upstairs.

Jake was in his room watching television. It was Saturday, and Saturdays meant Wayne slobbing out on the sofa for the whole day, with the remote control welded to his hand. Jake shared my opinion of Wayne and tended to keep out of the way. I leaned against the doorframe, watching him as he concentrated on Thunderbirds.

My heart swelled with love and pride as I watched his beautiful little face, his big blue eyes wide with wonder at the adventures unfolding on the screen before him. I wondered how it was possible to love someone so much, when he looked the image of the man who'd hurt us both so badly.

'Has it nearly finished?' I asked him.

Glancing up at me he nodded. 'Nearly. Can I have Thunderbird Three for Christmas, Mum?'

I smiled. 'Well, there's a few weeks to go yet, Jakey. You may change your mind, but we'll see. When the programme ends do you want to come out with me? I think we should take Baxter for a walk — get him away from Wayne and Maddie for a bit.'

He beamed at me. 'Yes please.'

'I've just got to make a phone call. Finish your programme then we'll get ready.'

I headed into my bedroom and rummaged in my bag for my mobile phone. Sitting on the bed, I scrolled through the list of entries in my contacts then paused, my finger hovering over Liam's name. My stomach churned at the thought of speaking to him, but I had no choice. It was for Jake I reminded myself.

Taking a deep breath, I pressed the call button and waited, my heart pounding, half hoping he wouldn't answer.

'Hello?'

'It's me, Ellie.'

'Yeah, I can read. What's up? Is Jakey all right?'

Well, that was a pleasant start to the conversation. I plucked nervously at a loose thread on my green cotton duvet cover. 'It depends what you mean by all right, I suppose.'

'Look, Ellie, if this is another call to try to make me feel guilty and beg me to come home, forget it. We're done. I'm with Laura now. Deal with it.'

A wave of anger swept my nerves aside. Who the hell did he think he was?

'Come home? Come home to where? In case you've forgotten, we haven't got a home any more, thanks to you and your bright ideas, not to mention your failure to save any money, despite all your promises.'

'I've not got time for this. Laura's waiting for me. We're going into town. Is there a point to this conversation?'

'I need some money.'

There, I'd said it. Was that to the point enough for him?

'Don't we all? What do you need it for?'

'I need a deposit for a flat or a house somewhere. I can't save much on my wages, and you owe me. You owe Jake. The least you can do is make sure he has a decent roof over his head.'

'What's wrong with Maddie's place?'

'She has a boyfriend now. She wants some privacy. You know as well as I do that this was only ever supposed to be temporary.'

'You should never have left my mother's. You were all right there. It's your own fault for being so stubborn.'

'My fault?' My hand tightened around my phone, my heart thudding as I fought down my rage. The injustice was almost too much to bear. 'Look, I'm not going to argue all day about this. Can you lend me some money for a deposit or not?'

'Not.'

'Are you joking? You must be able to lend me something?'

'Is that Ellie?'

My stomach did a cartwheel at Luscious Laura's voice in the background.

'What's she moaning about now?'

'Ellie, I've got to go.'

'You can't go yet. I need some help. I can't stay here much longer, and we have nowhere to go. I know you don't care about me, but you have a son here that needs a decent home.'

'Tell her we're going out,' demanded Laura. 'Come on, babes, it's nearly two o'clock now.'

'Ellie, I haven't got any money. I'm completely broke. I'd lend you some if I had any, but I haven't.'

'Is she after money?' Laura sounded outraged. 'Of all the nerve. She's working, isn't she? Tell her to tighten the purse strings. We've got enough to pay for. Weddings don't come cheap.'

'Weddings?' I croaked as my throat tightened. 'Did she just say weddings? Are you getting married?'

'Yeah, yeah. I was going to tell you. So, you see, I really don't have any cash spare. Have you thought of asking the council? They might give you a flat somewhere.'

'There's a waiting list a mile long, Liam, and besides, you know what their flats are like. I can't—'

'Babes, will you hurry up? We've got a wedding fayre to get to!'

'Coming, honey. Sorry, Ellie. Got to go, really. Get yourself to the council. They'll sort you out. Tell Jakey I'll see him next Sunday. Bye.'

The phone went dead. I stared at the screen as it switched back to a picture of Jake, smiling up at me with innocent eyes. So, that was the answer? Throw myself on the mercy of the council and pray that, if I was very lucky, they'd give me one of the empty high-rise flats on one of the town's estates? I knew what they were like. Lifts used as public toilets, hallways strewn with graffiti and rubbish, dodgy-looking youths lurking on landings.

I couldn't stand to live in one myself, never mind subjecting Jake to that environment. What now?

Numbly, I pulled on my trainers and found my coat. So, Liam and Laura were getting married. That hadn't taken them long. Amazing that he could find the money to pay for a wedding but couldn't spare anything to put a roof over his child's head. I felt a sudden bitterness and tried hard to let it go. Holding on to it wouldn't help. If it would provide a home for me and my son I'd have happily wallowed in it all day, but the cold fact was, no amount of bitterness, or pain, or anger would change the situation. I had to move on, and I also had to face facts. I wasn't going to get any help from anyone. I would have to sort things out for myself, and I would. I'd find a decent home for us, if it meant scouring every newspaper, every online property site…

If it meant moving away.

I paused. Would I move away? Leave the town where I'd grown up? It was all I knew. Could I really bring myself to leave? But then, what was there for me now? I had no family of my own left there, apart from Maddie, since my mum had moved to Spain after my dad died, and I could always make new friends. Maybe I could find a job that paid higher wages somewhere else. If it could give Jake a better life it would be worth the upheaval. Feeling a new determination, I headed back into Jake's room and was pleased to see him fastening his coat.

'Thunderbirds finished?'

He nodded. 'It was F.A.B. Where are we going?'

I shrugged and held out my hand for his. 'I'm not sure. The park? The woods? We'll see where our legs carry us, eh?'

He laughed and took my hand, and together we went downstairs. Wayne and Maddie looked up we entered the living room.

'Going out?' Maddie barely tried to keep the delight from her voice.

'Thought we'd take Baxter for a walk. He's obviously bored, and Jakey could do with some fresh air. You don't mind, do you?'

'Feel free,' said Maddie. 'You know where his lead is.'

'Yeah, and take your time,' said Wayne. 'No need to rush back.'

He and Maddie grinned at each other, and I ushered Jake into the kitchen, calling for Baxter as I did so. He appeared immediately, his whole demeanour changing as he realised he was about to get out of the house.

'I don't blame you, Baxter,' I whispered, as I clipped the lead to his collar. 'I can't wait to get out of here too. Looks like we've both outstayed our welcome.'

Chapter 3
A Walk in the Park

Baxter pulled hard on his lead. It took all my strength to restrain him, and I was out of breath by the time we reached the park.

'He's glad to be outside isn't he, Mum?' said Jake, laughing when Baxter snorted, apparently in full agreement.

'He certainly seems to be,' I agreed. I wondered exactly how much exercise the dog had been getting. Maddie ran a business from home, and she'd assured me she was taking him for regular walks, but I wasn't so sure. She'd certainly made no attempt to walk him that morning. Was she lying? Maybe that was why Baxter was being so naughty. He probably had loads of energy that wasn't getting used up.

'Are we going to feed the ducks?' Jake scanned the lake ahead of us. He loved the ducks. There was a small wooden shop at the side of the lake that sold duck food, among other things, and we'd gone there regularly since he was a toddler in his buggy to throw the mixture of grains, rice, and corn the park provided.

'Let's see if they have any food left,' I said.

I wondered uneasily what Baxter would make of the birds and automatically tightened my hold on the lead, but although he sniffed the air with curiosity, he seemed unfazed by their presence. He stood watching quite amiably as Jake scattered the feed for them.

As he did so my thoughts, despite my best efforts, kept straying back to the phone call. Liam was getting married again. How did that make me feel? Wretched, worthless, easily replaced. Yet did it really matter? So he was marrying Laura. He was already living with her, so what difference did a piece of paper and a ring make? It wasn't as if being married had made much difference to Liam's loyalty to me, was it? Why should Laura be able to trust him any more than I had? And I hadn't — not really. There'd always been a nagging voice, whispering a warning in my ear, right from the moment I'd met him.

He'd been so charming and attentive, but from the beginning there'd been something about him that made me uneasy. I'd always put my faith in my instincts until Liam, listening to the little voice that seemed to know whether someone could be trusted or not. It had whispered to me from the first that he was one of those people who kept secrets.

He was sly. I'd caught him out in his lies many, many times, yet he'd always seemed to have an explanation, and a way about him that made me laugh it off and forgive him. The good times had been really good, and had helped him fool me, but those times had grown fewer and further between.

I had to be honest with myself. The relationship had stopped being a rewarding one many years ago. I was better off out of it. I wondered why that knowledge didn't fully take away the pain. Sometimes I wished I'd never met Liam Jackson.

Jake giggled and threw the last of the food to the eager ducks. Baxter sat quietly beside us, watching the strange little creatures scrabbling for food with keen interest. Jake put the empty bag in his pocket and threw his arms around the dog.

'Good boy. He was very good wasn't he, Mum? He wasn't naughty to the ducks was he?'

I smiled down at him. He was so beautiful. How could I regret meeting Liam, however much he'd hurt me, when he'd given me such a wonderful child?

I ruffled Jake's dark hair and nodded. 'He was very good. Shall we let him have a run around as a reward?'

Jake clapped his hands. 'I'll race him. Can I race him, Mum?'

'Okay. Let's get away from the lake first shall we? We'll go over to the field. Come on.'

We headed over toward the far end of the park, Baxter pulling eagerly on his lead as if he sensed freedom was only moments away.

'Next time we should bring the Frisbee shouldn't we? Or a ball? Shall we do that next time?'

'I think that would be fun. I'm sure Baxter would like a game with you.' I reached down and unclipped

Baxter's lead. 'Okay, boy, off you go. Quick run around, burn off some of that excess energy.'

Jake whooped with delight as Baxter leapt forward. 'Race you, Baxter!' he yelled, running after the dog, his arms waving with excitement.

Baxter slowed, almost as if he were waiting for Jake to catch up, then they ran together across the field. I walked in their wake, laughing at their joyful exertions. It was good to see my little boy letting off steam. He'd had a rough time of it lately and he never complained. He'd obviously really taken to Baxter.

I frowned, chewing my lip as I thought about the future. I'd go online when I got home. Check out the flats and houses for rent again. Cast the net a bit wider. Jake was going to have a decent home, no matter what the cost.

They started running back towards me and I stood still, waiting. Jake's face was flushed, his eyes bright with laughter. Baxter could easily have outrun him, but he kept pace with my son, turning his head every now and then as if to check that Jake was still with him. If I hadn't known better, I'd have sworn the dog was smiling.

I threw open my arms and Jake ran into them. 'I won! I won didn't I?' he shouted.

'I think you did,' I said, then glanced round in alarm as Baxter charged past me.

'Baxter! Baxter, come here!'

He'd apparently decided that allowing Jake to win

the race was enough good behaviour for one day, and he streaked across the field with astonishing speed, weaving between children playing football, and ignoring a couple of other dogs who wanted him to stop and play.

I grabbed Jake's hand and we ran after him. I silently prayed that he wouldn't cause any trouble or head out of the park. I hoped he'd forgotten about the ducks.

Baxter had almost reached the other end of the field, where a man was busy texting on his mobile phone. He was wearing loose jogging pants and a sweatshirt and was evidently concentrating on his phone so much that he was totally oblivious to the missile heading his way. As I watched, he shoved his phone back in his pocket, crouched down suddenly and fumbled with his trainers, still blissfully unaware of the danger he was in.

Baxter cannoned right into him, and I yelped as the man fell flat on his back.

'Oh, no! Oh, God, Baxter, what have you done?'

By the time Jake and I reached them, Baxter was licking the man's face while he lay, seemingly winded, on the ground.

'I can't apologise enough. He gets a little over excited. It's the first time I've let him off the lead and I think he was on an adrenaline high because he'd just been racing Jake here. I don't think he meant to knock you over, but then you bent down you see, and he wouldn't have been able to stop, and… I'm so sorry.'

I peered down at the man, trying to decide if he looked angry enough to threaten to sue me. He blinked up at me, his face red, and I held my breath as he opened his mouth to reply. Before he could, Baxter slurped his face with his tongue. At one point, it was practically a French kiss, and I cringed, horrified.

'Baxter! Stop it now!'

Baxter took not the slightest bit of notice, but Jake ran to him, grabbed his collar, and managed to haul him away from the poor man, who rubbed his face looking a bit stunned.

'Ugh.'

Well at least he could speak. That was something. I'd feared that Baxter had knocked all the air out of his lungs. If he decided to make a fuss about it Maddie and Wayne would be furious. Baxter would be in even more bother and, of course, they would blame me. I couldn't afford a lawsuit.

'I'm so, so sorry.' I held out my hand to him and, after a moment's hesitation, he took it and allowed me to pull him to his feet. 'It's not his fault. He's had a tough time of it lately. He was abandoned by a cruel, heartless owner, and he's still trying to settle in. I know he didn't mean to hurt you. Are you all right?'

'Well I've been better,' he admitted and studied Baxter, who wagged his tail furiously. 'Sounds like he's had a rough deal.'

He sounded a bit shaky. I hoped he wasn't concussed.

'Oh, he has. He just needs to settle, that's all. He's not a bad dog, he's just over excited. He has a lot of energy and doesn't get to burn it off as much as he should.'

'Don't you take him for regular walks?'

'Well, he's not actually my dog...' I didn't quite know how to explain the situation, and my voice trailed off.

The man rubbed the back of his neck. He was younger than I'd realised, probably in his early thirties, and had a shock of brown hair and grey-green eyes. The baggy sweatshirt and jogging pants didn't do him any favours.

'Were you going for a run?' I asked him. 'I'm sorry we interrupted you.'

He shook his head. 'Oh, no, no. That's okay. I'm all done for today. I'm Dylan by the way.' He held out his hand and I took it, glad he was being civil and not threatening to call the police about my mad, uncontrollable dog.

'I'm Ellie, and this is my son, Jake. And this, as you probably heard, is Baxter.'

Dylan smiled at Jake then reached over and patted Baxter, who immediately took a leap forward, nearly pulling Jake over. I grabbed him and clipped his lead back on.

'Baxter the Boxer, eh? Catchy.'

He bent down and made a huge fuss of the dog, which was big of him, given the circumstances.

'You're a beauty, aren't you? Aren't you a handsome

boy? Yes, you are. Yes, you are.'

Baxter seemed thoroughly delighted with Dylan's opinion and made some very appreciative noises while his ears were rubbed, and his squashed black nose kissed.

'It's very good of you to be so understanding. Not many people would be.'

'I love dogs,' admitted Dylan. 'He didn't mean to knock me over. And if he's had a bad time of it… Did you say he's not your dog?'

I sighed. 'Sadly not. He belongs to my cousin. We live with her you see — at least, for the moment. She has a habit of taking in waifs and strays.'

The man raised an eyebrow and I hurried on, wondering why on earth I'd said such a thing.

'Poor Baxter here had been abandoned and—'

'Abandoned?' Dylan's head shot up. 'You mean he was a stray? But he's a pedigree Boxer dog. Surely—'

'Well no, he wasn't a stray. He was free to a good home but, to be honest, I don't think the good home bit mattered at all.'

'Oh? Why not?' He stroked Baxter's head again and then turned back to me. 'You think they'd have let just anyone have him?'

'They did,' I said grimly. 'Don't get me wrong, my cousin's lovely, but they didn't know that did they? They didn't check out our home or anything. If they'd made even the most basic enquiries, they'd have known that Maddie's never owned a dog in her life, and this was more about her feeling sorry for Baxter and acting on a whim than actually wanting to bring a dog into her life.'

'I can't believe it.' Dylan shook his head.

'I know. They didn't even send any of his things with him. Apparently this Melissa woman threw everything away, and Maddie had to go out and buy everything from scratch.'

'So he had nothing from his old home? Not even his bed? What about toys? Surely—'

'Nothing. The owner said they were dirty. Well, she wasn't the owner, she was the owner's girlfriend, and Maddie said she was horrible — a real princess type — but the owner is even worse in my opinion. He dumped the poor dog after five years because the girlfriend didn't like dogs. I mean, really! People like him don't deserve dogs. Don't you agree?'

'You're so right.' Dylan's gaze fell on his phone, still lying on the grass, and he bent to retrieve it. 'The man's clearly a moron. I hope he feels racked with guilt,' he finished, shoving the phone in his pocket.

'Poor Baxter couldn't settle, and of course, he didn't even have anything with the scent of home on it to help him. Between you and me,' I whispered, seeing as Jake had become preoccupied with teaching Baxter to give him his paw, 'he wouldn't sleep on the new bed, and I found him lying on my cousin's best jumper, so I've been letting him sleep in my bedroom. Maddie would kill me if she knew but, bless him, he needs company.'

'That's very good of you.'

Dylan gazed into my eyes and smiled. He had a nice smile. I could feel myself blushing.

'Baxter's very lucky to have you. Dogs like him need lots of time and attention to stop them getting bored. He'll be quite destructive if he doesn't get the love and exercise that he needs.'

'You're obviously a dog lover,' I said.

He nodded. 'Definitely. I come to this park a lot to walk my dog. We love it here. He sits with me while I feed the ducks, and he has a good run on this field, and sometimes we go to the woods too. Although I've got to watch him there. Daren't let him off the lead, because if he scents a rabbit he's off.' He laughed, and his hand reached out for Baxter's head again.

'We've just fed the ducks haven't we, Mum?' said Jake. 'And Baxter was really good too. What's your dog called?' he asked.

Dylan smiled. 'My dog? He's called Tyson.'

'Tyson? Is he another Boxer?' I laughed.

'Why isn't he with you?' enquired Jake.

'Well I'm jogging.' Dylan shrugged.

'Doesn't matter. Tyson could jog with you,' said Jake. 'Baxter ran with me. I beat him though,' he confided.

Dylan laughed. 'Wow! You must run very fast then. But when I'm jogging I like to concentrate. I take my running very seriously, young man. Tyson needs my full attention, so it wouldn't be fair on either of us.'

'Would you like to join us tomorrow?'

Honestly, I could have clapped my hand over my mouth, blurting that out. He'd think I was mad, and perhaps I was. It wasn't like me to ask a total stranger on a date. What was I talking about? It wasn't a date. I just wanted company — for Baxter.

As Dylan stared back at me steadily, saying nothing, I wilted under the gaze from those soft grey-green eyes.

'Sorry. You're not likely to want to join us, are you? Not after Baxter's behaviour.'

Yeah, put the blame on Baxter. Never mind my own weird behaviour.

He smiled suddenly. 'I think that's a great idea. It does get a bit boring, walking Tyson alone every day, and it would be good for Baxter to socialise with other dogs. What time?'

I shrugged, trying to look casual. 'It's Sunday. Any time will be fine by me.'

He considered. 'I can't get away too early tomorrow. Would eleven be all right? Normally it would be earlier, but weekends are tricky.'

'Eleven would be perfect.' Realising how broadly I beamed at him, I tried to straighten my face. He'd think I was a complete lunatic at the rate I was going. Perhaps I was. Perhaps the shock of Liam's impending marriage, my perilous living arrangements, and my worries about my financial situation were taking their toll on my nerves.

Dylan was grinning too though, and I relaxed a little. What did it matter? I was only asking a perfect stranger to accompany me and my son, and our rather boisterous dog, on a walk around the park. I hadn't proposed had I?

'Tomorrow at eleven. It's a date,' he said. 'See you tomorrow, boy,' he added, giving Baxter one last pat. 'And you too, Jake. Very nice to meet you,' he said, shaking my son's hand.

Jake looked delighted to be treated in such a grownup fashion. 'Bye, Dylan. See you tomorrow.'

Dylan turned and began to jog slowly away from us. Baxter tried to follow but I pulled him back, with some effort. 'Oh, no you don't! That's quite enough from you for today, thank you very much.'

We watched Dylan running through the park gates, and I took a deep breath and turned back to Jake.

'Right, well. Now all that excitement's over, let's get Baxter home, shall we?'

Jake wrinkled his nose. 'S'pose so. Will Wayne still be there?'

'Probably. You don't like him much, do you?'

'Not really. Can I go upstairs and watch telly?'

I hesitated. 'Tell you what, how about we drop Baxter back home and then go into town? We could have a look at those Thunderbirds toys at the toy shop. Get some ideas for your Christmas list.'

'Really? And can we have a milkshake at the burger

bar?'

I grinned and ruffled his hair. 'Why not?'

'Hear that, Baxter? I'm going into town with Mum. It's a shame Baxter can't come with us, isn't it?'

'Hmm.' Frankly, I thought a break from Baxter would be quite welcome. I'd had quite enough of his escapades for one afternoon. Then again, if he hadn't had a rush of energy I would never have met Dylan, and he seemed a nice, friendly sort of man. There were so many difficulties in my life now, it would be a pleasure to be around someone so completely uncomplicated.

Chapter 4
The Tortoise and the Hare

'You've been letting Baxter sleep in your bedroom, haven't you?' Maddie's tone was accusing, and I knew there was little point in trying to deny it.

'He wouldn't settle downstairs. He was crying. I felt sorry for him, and he's been no trouble at all.'

'Huh! Apart from all the dog hairs on the bedroom carpet. That was new last year, you know.'

'They'll soon clean up. I'll run the vacuum cleaner over them in a minute.' I frowned as a thought occurred to me. 'What were you doing in my bedroom?'

Maddie scowled. 'Er, I think you'll find it's *my* bedroom, actually. I was just checking the boiler, that's all.'

I raised an eyebrow. 'Really? Why?'

'It was making a funny noise. Anyway, that's not the point. I don't want that dog upstairs. It's my house, and those are my rules.'

I nodded. 'Fair enough. It won't happen again.'

'Good.' Maddie flounced out of the room, but not

43

before I'd caught the scent of my own perfume. I had a feeling she'd borrowed it before, as the bottle had emptied surprisingly quickly, and I hadn't worn any for a while. There was no point confronting Maddie about it though. She would only deny it, and it would cause yet another scene. There'd been more than enough of those lately.

I closed my laptop with a sigh. There was nothing affordable on the property sites I'd been checking out for the last hour, and all I'd achieved was to make myself feel even more dispirited. Time to cheer myself up.

I glanced at my watch. I just had time to vacuum the bedroom carpet then Jake and I could get Baxter's lead and escape to the park. It occurred to me that the situation really had sunk to an all-time low if I considered getting out of the house an escape. How had things got so bad?

Maddie and I used to be very close, even as children. Sharing a house for the last six months had taken its toll on our friendship, and I felt sad about that. Having Wayne around, making his sarcastic comments and urging Maddie to get rid of her unwanted guests, wasn't helping the situation. Maybe I would have to approach the council after all.

I collected the vacuum cleaner from the cupboard under the stairs and dragged it up to my bedroom, warning Jake that we'd be leaving very soon, and he'd better get his shoes and coat on before I plugged it in.

He was ready before I'd even finished vacuuming, obviously as keen as I was to get out of the house.

Baxter, who'd been curled up under the kitchen table looking extremely sorry for himself, nearly knocked a chair over in his eagerness when we approached, his lead dangling from my hand.

'Come on then and no misbehaving today,' I warned, as I opened the back door.

'Do you think he'll be all right with Tyson?' asked Jake, as we set off for the park. 'Some dogs don't like other dogs do they?'

'He didn't bother with those loose dogs that wanted to play yesterday did he?' I reassured him. 'And he was so good with the ducks, I can't see there being a problem.'

The park was busy. It was a cold but dry Sunday morning, and there were lots of people around. I noted the number of children accompanied only by their fathers and wondered how many were on access visits. Liam saw Jake every other Sunday — his choice. I'd never raised an objection about access, realising our son needed his father, but what had started out as visits to Liam and Laura's house every weekend had dwindled to every Sunday, and had eventually dropped to every other Sunday. Liam always had a reason, and I couldn't exactly force him could I?

While Jake said very little on the subject, I worried endlessly about the effect it was all having on him. He didn't deserve any of it. I wondered why Liam couldn't see what a wonderful son he had, and why he didn't want to spend every possible moment in his company.

'He's not here is he, Mum? Do you think he'll come?' Jake's face was anxious, and I ruffled his hair, trying to quell my own concerns.

I didn't want yet another man to let Jake down but, on the other hand, Dylan was hardly a friend was he? I couldn't exactly hold him to anything, and I had to make sure my son realised it had only been a casual arrangement.

'Dylan? Oh well, he may. It doesn't really matter does it? We're here to walk Baxter. If Dylan turns up that's very nice, but if he doesn't we'll still have a good time won't we?'

'But he said he'd come. He will come won't he? He said Baxter could meet Tyson.'

I closed my eyes and took a deep breath. 'Sometimes people say things, Jake. It doesn't mean they're deliberately lying, just that other things come up. Dylan did say that weekends are tricky for him, remember? He may have wanted to come, but something cropped up that he couldn't get out of.'

'Like Dad?'

'Dad?'

'Yeah.' Jake kicked a clump of turf and shrugged. 'Sometimes, Dad says he'll pick me up, but then things happen, and he can't.'

I swallowed, my heart breaking for him. 'Yes, a bit like that. Except, we hardly know Dylan, and we can't really be cross with him if he can't make it, can we?'

'I'm not cross. I'm just…' Jake's voice trailed off and he sighed. Not for the first time, I found myself wanting to go round to Liam's house and scream at him. He had no idea of the damage he'd done.

As if he sensed my sudden anger, Baxter stood to attention, every muscle tensing.

'It's okay, Baxter,' said Jake, patting the dog's head. 'What is it? What are you — oh!' He started to giggle, and I stared in amazement as I spotted Dylan strolling towards us.

Trotting beside him was a tiny little Yorkshire terrier with a red ribbon in its hair. That was Tyson?

'Morning! Sorry I'm a bit late.'

In jeans and wearing a brown leather jacket over a cream Arran jumper, he looked much taller than he had yesterday, somehow, and leaner. I tried very, very hard not to stare at him.

Baxter seemed torn, his head swinging between Dylan, who he was obviously delighted to see again, and the little dog, who was evidently crying out for further investigation.

'This is Tyson?' I nodded at the little terrier and tried not to laugh, unlike Jake who was openly finding the revelation highly amusing.

'Yeah, yeah.' Dylan ran his hand through his thick, brown hair and shrugged, obviously embarrassed. 'It's a joke. An affectionate nickname 'cos of his size. Don't be fooled, though. He's a terrier, and terriers are tough little chaps.'

'If you say so.'

I groaned as Baxter made up his mind what his priority was and launched himself at Dylan, his paws landing hard on the poor man's stomach.

'Ouch! Okay, Baxter, I'm pleased to see you too.' Dylan laughed and fussed the dog, handing Tyson's lead to Jake with some relief, as it became apparent that Baxter would settle for nothing less than his new friend's full attention.

'He really likes you,' said Jake.

'Does he? He hides it well.' Dylan managed to prise Baxter off him eventually and, almost reluctantly, the dog turned to greet Tyson. The two of them sniffed each other curiously for a few minutes, circling each other and getting their leads quite tangled in the process.

I noted, with huge relief, that they seemed quite friendly with each other, and Tyson didn't seem at all fazed by Baxter's size.

'Shall we let them have a run together?' suggested Dylan.

'You think they'll be okay?'

'Yes, no problem. It will do them good to burn off some energy. Watch Tyson try to outrun Baxter. I'll guarantee it.'

'He'll never do that,' said Jake scornfully.

'Maybe not, but he'll try,' said Dylan with some confidence. 'He may have the body of a Yorkshire terrier, but he's got the heart of a lion. Watch him go.'

We unclipped the leads and howled with laughter as Tyson immediately streaked across the field, taking Baxter — who was too busy licking Dylan's hand to notice — totally by surprise. Once he'd realised what was happening he looked stunned, then he galloped after the little dog, as if determined not to be humiliated.

'Told you,' Dylan said smugly. 'He never gives up and always takes him by surprise.'

'Him?'

'Whichever dog he's racing. They underestimate him. Kind of like the tortoise and the hare. So, young man…' Dylan turned toward Jake and rummaged in his jacket pocket. 'How do you fancy an ice cream? The shop seems to be doing a roaring trade in them, despite the weather,' he added, nodding at a bunch of eager children, clustered round the little wooden tuck shop by the lake. 'Here's some money. Get a chocolate flake and some sprinkles on it.'

Jake looked delighted. 'Can I, Mum?'

'Yes, of course, but you must come straight back. Where are your manners?'

'Thanks, Dylan.'

'My pleasure. Did you want one, Ellie?'

When Dylan smiled at me, my tummy fluttered in a very disturbing manner.

'No thanks, too cold for me, but I appreciate the offer. Shall we sit here on this bench?'

He nodded and we sat together, watching in silence for some moments as Jake headed off to the shop, and Tyson and Baxter galloped around the field.

'Quite impressive, isn't he?' I said, at last, nodding at the dogs. 'Tyson, I mean. Those little legs are working overtime to keep up with Baxter.'

'Baxter's playing with him. When the time's right he'll teach him a lesson and leave him way behind.'

I stared at him. 'What makes you think that?'

Dylan shrugged. 'They always do. Tyson likes to challenge big dogs, but they seem to find him amusing and always end up beating him, no matter how he tries.'

'But he keeps trying,' I murmured. 'I like that about him. No matter that the odds are stacked against him he still believes that one day he'll win the race.'

Dylan's expression softened as he studied my face. 'Sounds like you're in a race yourself, and not one you're confident of winning.'

I shook my head, embarrassed. 'Sorry. I don't know what made me say that. It's been a tough year.'

'I'm sorry to hear that. Still,' he gave me a smile that melted my heart like ice cream on a hot July day, 'you have Jake. That's got to be worth something.'

'It's worth everything. Believe me, he's what keeps me going. Do you have children?'

'Me?' Dylan laughed. 'I'm barely fit to keep a dog.'

His laughter died and he sighed suddenly. 'I'm an irresponsible idiot most of the time.'

'Oh? I find that hard to believe.'

I realised it was true. The little voice in my head was murmuring that he was a decent, caring sort of person. But then, what did I know about him really? Unlike Liam, at least Dylan had the guts to admit he wasn't perfect.

'You seem to have quite a bond with Tyson anyway, so you must be doing something right, and Baxter adores you. He's a very good judge of character. He hides when Maddie's boyfriend comes round.'

'Why does he do that? Christ, he doesn't hit him does he?'

A look of concern crossed Dylan's face, and I quickly shook my head.

'Oh, no, nothing like that. Just, he's not keen on dogs and I think Baxter senses it. Wayne thinks Maddie shouldn't have been so soft as to take him in. Or us, come to that. We're in his way too, and he wants us gone.'

'But Maddie wouldn't listen to him, surely?'

'I think Maddie wants us gone too. We've kind of outstayed our welcome. By about six months actually.'

'How long have you been living with her?'

I gave him a wry look. 'About six months.'

He raised an eyebrow then we both started to laugh.

'I don't know why I'm laughing,' I said, wiping my eyes after a moment. 'Things are pretty dire, and it's far from funny.'

'How come you're living with her anyway?' asked Dylan, then held up his hands in horror. 'Sorry!

Crossed a line there. You don't have to tell me anything. It's none of my business.'

I watched Baxter and Tyson for a moment. Beside me, Dylan's laughter broke through when Tyson began to yap in protest as Baxter streaked away from him, easily outrunning the little dog whose tiny legs were simply not up to the job.

'Told you,' he said. 'Happens every time. Poor Tyson, he never learns.'

'He will. One day.' I felt overwhelmed with sadness suddenly and was grateful when Dylan's hand rested on mine momentarily.

'Sorry,' he said, removing it almost immediately. 'Just, you looked so miserable, and I can see you've got an awful lot going on.'

He looked awkward, and I tried to pull myself together and make light of the situation.

'A messy divorce, that's all. Happens to a lot of people at some point or other.'

'Tell me about it.' His voice was loaded with feeling.

'You've been through it too?'

'Not directly. Never been married. My parents got divorced when I was very young. It was horrendous. They were both still full of bitterness towards each other, even years later, and my childhood was pretty much ruined by their petty games and quarrelling. They should never have got married in the first place. Mind you, I think that's pretty much true of everyone. Marriage is a cunning plan to destroy everyone's lives if you ask me.'

He seemed to expect me to agree but I couldn't.

'They obviously really hurt you. You must know someone who's happily married?'

He considered a moment. 'Yeah, a few people. But then it's still early days. Give it a couple of years and we'll see how happy they are then.'

'What an awful way to look at the world!'

He looked surprised. 'Don't you agree?'

'Certainly not! I think marriage can be the most wonderful thing that can happen to a person. You just have to meet the right one, that's all.'

'Sure. It's a great institution, but then—'

'Who want to live in an institution?' I finished for him, and he laughed.

'Okay, it's an oldie but goodie. Oh, hello Baxter. You've had enough running around for now then?'

Baxter plonked his head on Dylan's knee and gazed up at him adoringly, while I tried very hard not to feel offended that he was completely ignoring me. From across the way, Jake walked towards us, licking his ice cream. He raised a hand and waved to me, and I waved back, feeling the familiar surge of love for him.

'He really does mean the world to you doesn't he?' Dylan's voice was quiet, and I glanced at him, surprised.

'Of course he does. He's my son.'

'It doesn't necessarily follow.' He stroked Baxter's head for a moment, not adding to his statement, then stood up. 'Come on, Tyson,' he called. 'You've let the side down enough, don't you think? Get back here now.'

Tyson ignored the command, stopping to investigate a game of football that two young children were playing. Dylan called again, but Tyson may as well have been stone deaf for all the notice he took of him.

'Not very well trained is he?' said Jake, sitting between us on the bench. 'Thanks for the ice cream. It's lovely.'

'Pleasure, mate. And I can assure you, Tyson usually does as he's told every time. Can't understand it. Must be all the excitement.'

'Yeah, right!' Jake's eyes twinkled with mischief.

'Are you saying you don't believe me? That's outrageous! Tyson, come here now!'

Tyson yapped excitedly and began to nudge the football away from a little boy, who promptly howled.

'Oy, mate! Is this your dog? Get it on a lead, will you? My lads are trying to play football here!'

The child's father motioned for Dylan to collect Tyson, and rather shame-faced he went over to the little dog and clipped his lead back on.

'How embarrassing,' he confided, returning to the bench with the terrier in tow. 'Bad enough that he wouldn't behave, but now everyone knows I'm the proud owner of a Yorkshire terrier.'

'Well, you chose him didn't you?' I said, surprised.

'What? Oh, no. No. He, er, needed a home, and…'

He swallowed. 'I guess I'm a sucker for a waif and stray too.'

We looked at each other a moment then I turned away.

'Have you finished that ice cream, Jakey? How about we wander over to the playground, and you can go on the swings and slide for a while?'

'Are you coming, too?' Jake asked Dylan eagerly.

Dylan seemed to hesitate before smiling. 'Sure, why not? I'm sure your mum could cope with two dogs for a while. I'll race you to the slide!'

Chapter 5
Hot Chocolate and Cookies

The car door slammed, and I peered anxiously out of the window to see Jake standing on the kerb. I watched him wave as his father's car headed down the road. A lump formed in my throat as he hitched up his backpack and turned resolutely towards the house.

Switching on a bright smile, I hurried to the front door and opened it.

'You're back!' After standing aside to let him into the hallway, I hastily shut the door again as an excited Baxter bounded up to us, his tail wagging furiously.

'Did you have a nice day?' I asked, eyeing him anxiously as I helped him take off his backpack.

He seemed okay. His face didn't bear the usual tight, strained look that it wore most Sunday evenings, as he struggled to reassure me that he was fine, and he'd had a lovely day with his dad and Laura.

'It was okay. Laura made me a cake. Well, it was out of a packet, but she still had to put it in the oven, and it was nice, and they let me have three slices.'

He grinned at Baxter and threw his arms around the excited dog. 'Hello, boy! Did you miss me? I missed you!'

'A cake, eh? That was nice of her.' I hesitated, wondering if they'd broken the news to him about their forthcoming marriage. How would Jake react when he discovered Luscious Laura was about to be his new stepmother? 'Did — did they say anything else?' I tried not to sound anxious, but it was difficult.

Jake screwed up his face as if thinking. 'Oh, yeah! Dad's coming to watch me in the carol concert, so he wants you to get him a ticket. That's good isn't it?'

I struggled to hide my shock. Since Liam had about as much Christmas spirit as Ebenezer Scrooge and had always insisted we close the curtains and ignore the carol singers at the door every December, I hadn't for a moment expected that he'd agree to attend the event.

The school was hosting a carol concert during the first week of December to help raise money for next year's outings. I'd always turned up alone for school events in the past, and I felt quite sick for a moment, imagining how awkward it would feel to have to sit beside my ex-husband.

I pushed the feeling aside. I was being ridiculous and very selfish. If Liam wanted to spend additional time with Jake, that could only be a good thing. Jake certainly seemed to think so anyway.

'That's very kind of him,' I said. 'Isn't he at work that evening?'

'No. He said he'll take the night off, just for me.'

Jake looked quite proud of that, and I smiled. 'Well,

I should hope so too. We'll have to make sure you get extra practice then, won't we?'

'I'm going to tell Dylan. Do you think he'll come too?'

'I should think he'll be busy,' I said hastily. 'Besides, Dylan doesn't have children, so he probably doesn't bother with carol concerts much, to be honest.'

Jake nodded and headed into the living room, Baxter trotting beside him. 'Where's Wayne?' he whispered.

I winked. 'Gone home already. They had a bit of a tiff.'

'Good,' said Jake. 'Where's Maddie then?'

'In the kitchen,' I said. 'She's making our dinner. Are you hungry?'

Considering he'd had three slices of cake, I suspected probably not, but he nodded eagerly and said, 'Yeah. Starving. I only had a banana sandwich for lunch.'

'And three slices of cake!'

'That was this morning, for breakfast.'

Jake rushed into the kitchen, with me and Baxter following. Baxter sniffed appreciatively at the smell of roast chicken, and Jake imitated him perfectly.

'Hi, Maddie! That smells lovely.'

Maddie, busy mashing potatoes in a bowl, paused in her efforts and smiled at him. 'I hope you're hungry. There are extra large portions because Wayne's had to go home. Did you have a nice time at your dad's?'

Jake nodded. 'Yeah. He's coming to see me in the carol concert.'

'Is he?' Maddie raised an eyebrow at me, and I shrugged. 'Well, that's good of him isn't it?'

'Yeah. Oh, and Dad and Laura are getting married.'

Maddie and I exchanged glances. I hadn't mentioned my discovery to my cousin, having spent little time in her company recently.

For the first time in ages, Maddie looked like her old self, full of concern for me. 'That's nice. Why don't you go upstairs and wash your hands while I finish making dinner?'

'Okay.' Jake turned and left the kitchen, Baxter trailing him like a shadow.

'Don't let that dog upstairs!' called Maddie then turned to me. 'Are you okay, Ellie? Did you know about this?'

'Yes. It's fine. I've come to terms with it all now. If that's what Liam wants, let him have it. What difference does it make to me? Whether he and Laura stay together or not, there's no going back for us.'

'I'm sorry, I really am. It must still feel like a kick in the teeth. He's an idiot. She's just a stupid, vain kid. She'll get sick of him soon enough; you wait and see.'

I nodded. 'Probably. I was more worried about how Jakey would take it, but he doesn't seem at all bothered. I suppose that's a good thing.'

'Are you upset that Liam's going to the carol concert? That's a turn up for the books! Never thought he'd put himself out like that.'

'Me neither. I admit, I feel a bit weird about it. But then, Jake sees so little of him. I can't help but feel it's a good thing that Liam wants to spend more time with him. Maybe he has missed him after all.'

'Let's just hope he doesn't let him down,' said Maddie. 'Right, let's get on with this dinner. You couldn't strain the veg for me could you? Honestly, you need to be an octopus to cook a Sunday roast. Whose bright idea was this anyway?'

'Wayne's,' I said.

We looked at each other and burst out laughing. For a short while, it was as if the arguments and tension of the last few weeks had never happened.

***

'A carol concert, eh, Jakey?' said Dylan. 'In my day I was a dab hand at singing carols. We used to go around the houses, knocking on all our neighbours' doors, demanding money in exchange for a few lines of Good King Wenceslas.' He laughed. 'Funnily enough, we didn't make much. One year, me and my brother took four hours to make the grand sum of ninety-seven pence. We bought a chocolate bar and shared it on the way home.'

'Your brother?' I said, surprised. 'I didn't realise you had siblings.'

'Well, that's probably because I haven't mentioned

him until now,' said Dylan with a grin.

I blushed. Of course he hadn't. Why would he have? Honestly, it wasn't as if we'd had any in depth discussions was it?

'So, you have a brother?'

'Yep.' Dylan zipped up his jacket. 'Is it me, or has the weather taken a turn for the worse?'

Jake looked up from where he sat on the grass, playing with Baxter and Tyson. 'Can I get an ice cream, Mum?'

I stared at him. 'An ice cream?' I'd just been wishing I'd worn a thicker jumper under my coat, and he wanted ice cream? 'Are you insane? It's freezing.'

Dylan grinned. 'How about a hot chocolate, instead? With lots of marshmallows and a big swirl of whipped cream. The shop's been selling loads of them, from what I've seen.'

Jake looked delighted. 'Ooh, that sounds even better.'

'I'd better get it for you,' I told him. 'Don't want you spilling it all over yourself.'

'I'll go,' Dylan said immediately. 'Would you like one too, Ellie?'

I hesitated then smiled. 'Why not?'

'Three hot chocolates coming right up,' he said, as he jumped up from the bench.

'He's really nice isn't he?' Jake asked, plonking himself next to me and patting Baxter's head as we watched Dylan heading over to the shop.

'He is,' I confirmed. 'I think we've made a lovely new friend there, Jakey.'

The hot chocolates were huge, piled high with swirls of whipped cream and loads of mini marshmallows. My mouth watered just looking at them.

'Be careful, Jake,' Dylan said. 'It's very hot. I'd put it on the bench for a while to cool off, okay?'

Jake nodded and sighed. 'Hope it's not too long,' he said. 'I'm starving.'

Dylan and I exchanged glances. I'd just spotted two children coming out of the shop carrying giant cookies in their hands. No doubt Jake had seen them too. Dylan winked at me.

'Well, the shop does sell these amazing cookies,' he said slowly. 'I don't suppose you fancy one of those do you?' he asked.

'That would be great,' Jake said, jumping up.

I grinned and reached for my bag.

'Let me,' Dylan said, reaching into his jacket pocket for change.

'Oh no, honestly. You always pay. I'll get him one.'

Dylan shook his head. 'It's my treat. There you go, Jakey.'

Jake looked uncertainly at me, and I nodded. 'It's okay, Jakey. You can take it.'

'Thanks, Dylan.' Jake took the coins and rushed off to the shop.

Baxter and Tyson seemed about to follow him, but

Dylan was prepared and grabbed hold of their collars. 'Oh no you don't! Come on, sit here.'

The two dogs sat patiently, allowing themselves to be stroked and fussed for a while, while our hot chocolates cooled on the bench beside us.

'So,' I said, seizing the chance to find out a little more about Dylan while I had the opportunity, 'your brother?'

'What about him?' He picked up his drink and prodded at the whipped cream.

'Well, do you have more than one? Sisters? Older, or younger?'

Dylan laughed. 'Why do I feel like I'm being interviewed?'

I blushed, and he nudged me. 'Only joking. I don't have any sisters. I just have one brother, who's three years younger than me and never lets me forget it. He's married with a four-year-old daughter. She's in the nursery class at Jake's school actually.'

'Really? Hmm. So, your brother's three years younger than you and already has a child in nursery? You have a lot of catching up to do!'

I could have died with embarrassment as I realised what I'd said. He would think I was propositioning him at that rate. Was I? Of course not! I was just having a friendly chat with a nice man. That was all. *Yes, keep telling yourself that, Ellie,* I thought grimly.

'Hmm. She'll probably have a child of her own before I feel able to have kids,' said Dylan.

'Really? Why are you so against having children? You're awfully good with Jake. I think you'd make a great father.'

Oh hell, I'd done it again. I ought to have a zip on that mouth of mine.

'That's what Greg says. He's my brother. He and his wife are always banging on at me to settle down and have kids.'

'But you don't want any?'

'I just think kids deserve the best, and I'm not sure I'd be up to the job.' He shrugged.

'So, your brother and his wife are still together? Well, there's an example of a happily married couple for you!'

'Who said they were happy?' His eyes twinkled. 'No, to be fair, they're really good together. In fact, they're so happy it's sickening, but I really don't think they're typical. When I think of married couples, I don't think of them, I think of — other people.'

'Like your parents?' I said gently. Obviously, his parents' divorce had affected him badly. Enough to put him off ever marrying or having children of his own, it seemed, which I thought was a real shame and, quite frankly, a terrible waste of a good-looking, decent man.

'My parents didn't have a marriage. They had a war. Even after the divorce there was no surrender. Greg and I weren't children, we were grenades to be hurled between them to inflict as much damage on the enemy as possible. Oh, well, Dad's dead now, and Mum's living somewhere down south with her latest fella. It doesn't matter anymore.'

Jake came running back, cookie in hand, so I said nothing else on the subject, but I couldn't stop thinking about how hurt and bewildered those two little boys must have been throughout their childhood. God forbid Jake should ever feel like that. I'd do everything in my power to keep things civil with Liam, no matter how much he'd hurt me.

'You have whipped cream on your nose,' Dylan said.

'What? Oh!' I blushed, as he reached over and gently dabbed at the end of my nose. I noticed the gold flecks in his eyes, and that he had rather long eyelashes. I swallowed.

'Oh, no you don't!' Jake whisked his hand away quickly, as Baxter made a lunge for the cookie. Unfortunately, as he moved it to the other side of his body, Tyson took a gamble and leapt up, managing to knock the biscuit from Jake's hand.

'Tyson!' All three of us yelled, and the little dog jumped, licking his lips guiltily. Baxter looked quite put out that he'd failed where his tiny pal had succeeded.

'Well, it seems to be quite tasty,' I said with a wry smile, watching both dogs eagerly wolfing down the remains of the cookie. 'You'd better buy another one. Here,' I said, handing him the money.

Jake rushed back to the shop, and the two dogs sniffed around, looking for any biscuit they'd missed.

'Can't believe you did that,' said Dylan, shaking his head at Tyson, as he sat, busily licking crumbs from the fur around his mouth. 'You look so sweet and innocent and you're nothing but a thief.'

'A cute thief, though,' I pointed out. I reached out and stroked Tyson, who immediately rolled over to have his belly tickled. I laughed and began to tickle him then stopped, my eyes widening. 'Er, Dylan…'

He followed my gaze and was silent for a moment. 'Oh.'

'Oh, indeed. I thought you said Tyson was a boy? Quite clearly, she's a girl.' Dylan swallowed, then put his fingers to his lips. 'Shh, she'll hear you.'

'Who'll hear me?'

'Tyson! She doesn't know, you see. She thinks she's a boy.'

I wondered if he'd gone mad.

'What the heck are you talking about?'

'She doesn't realise she's a girl. She'd be ever so upset if she knew the truth, so we let her think she's a boy. Hence the name.'

'And how do you know all this?'

'Well, let's just say she wouldn't be interested in Baxter in any romantic fashion.'

Screwing up my nose as Baxter's thick tongue busily licked crumbs from his squashed face, I couldn't help wondering how many lady dogs would. 'You mean she's gay? You're saying you have a gay dog?'

'That's right.'

'I don't know what to say to that,' I admitted.

'I hope you're not homophobic,' said Dylan, in mock indignation.

'I'm just stunned. I don't think I've ever met a gay dog before. Especially a gay dog who doesn't know it's gay but thinks it's a member of the opposite sex. Interesting.'

'I'm glad I've broadened your education,' said Dylan.

I couldn't help laughing. I had no idea what he was talking about, but at least he'd relaxed and was smiling again. He'd lost all the tension that had been in his face when he'd talked about his parents. He looked a different person, and I realised that he was extraordinarily handsome when he smiled, and that I wanted to see him smile much more. Inside my head, my little voice whispered that beside me, at last, was a man who might put the smile back on my own face too.

Chapter 6
A Close Encounter

I'd just pulled the wheelie bin back into the garden, and was closing the gate, when I heard the commotion coming from the kitchen. Wondering what on earth had happened, I slid the bolt into place and headed back indoors, where I found Wayne, the vein in his forehead almost popping with rage, waving a pair of jeans at Baxter.

In response the dog sprawled under the table, seeming not particularly bothered. It was as if he'd realised that Wayne was all hot air, and he no longer concerned himself with his temper tantrums. I rather admired him for it.

Maddie hung onto Wayne's arm in a vain attempt to soothe him. She wasn't having much success by the look of it. I watched in fascination as the vein throbbed and pulsed. How much longer could it continue before it burst, I wondered?

I was glad Jake was at school and didn't have to witness such a display.

'What the heck are you shouting for?' I asked him. 'I could hear you all the way from the end of the garden.'

'That dog! Look what that dog's done now!' Wayne turned an accusing eye on me, as if it was all my fault and Baxter was my responsibility. Although, come to think of it, he seemed to be more and more my responsibility lately.

I was the one who fed him, cleaned his teeth, and made sure he had fresh water, and I was certainly responsible for taking him for walks. Maddie hadn't made the slightest attempt to, for over a week at least. The novelty had well and truly worn off, and I was certain it was only guilt that had prevented her from seeking a new home for poor Baxter. It was guilt that prevented her from coming right out and telling me and Jake to leave too, no doubt.

Well, with any luck, it wouldn't be long before we could. I'd seen a flat advertised, and the rent was just about affordable. What was more, the owner wasn't demanding an arm and a leg as a deposit. The only downside was, there were no pets allowed. What would happen to Baxter once we left?

As if sensing my thoughts, Baxter edged his way out from under the table and made his way slowly to my side. I crouched down beside him, my arms going around him protectively.

'What's he done?'

'Are you blind? My jeans. Look at my jeans!' Wayne waved the jeans in my face, and I frowned.

'Can't see anything wrong with them.'

'The pocket's torn off. Look at that!'

'Is that all? That can easily be mended.'

'And there's slobber and paw prints all over them!'

'They can be washed.' I scowled at him. 'Honestly, what a fuss about nothing.'

'Do you know how much these jeans cost me? They're not your average market tat, you know. These are designer jeans. They cost me nearly three hundred quid.'

'Three hundred pounds for a pair of jeans?' I bit my lip before I could be tempted to tell him what an idiot he was for forking out that much for a few scraps of denim. 'How did Baxter get hold of them?'

'They were on my bedroom floor. He shouldn't have been in there. That's your fault,' said Maddie accusingly. 'You've trained him to go upstairs, by letting him sleep in your room. I told you not to do it.'

'And I haven't,' I protested. 'Not since you mentioned it.'

'Greedy git,' said Wayne, glaring at the dog fiercely. 'I know what you were after, mate. You knew my mints were in my pocket, didn't you? And you snaffled the lot, paper, an' all. Well, you can forget about having any tea tonight.'

'Don't be ridiculous,' I snapped. 'You can't not feed him, just because he had a few mints. That's cruelty.'

'And eating my best jeans isn't? I should sue you.'

'Sue me? He's not my dog!'

'May as well be.' Maddie sniffed. 'He never bothers

with me does he? Only ever wants you.'

'Is it surprising? You either ignore him or yell at him. Why would he want to be around you? You should never have taken him on. You have no idea about caring for dogs, and you're obviously not interested in him.'

'I was trying to do something nice!' Maddie yelled. 'That's all the thanks I get. Well, I won't be so soft in the future, you can bet on that. I've learned my lesson about doing favours for people, and for animals. Wish I'd never bothered with either of you. The sooner you both go the better!'

I flinched. Maddie looked immediately uncomfortable, obviously realising she'd gone a step too far. She shrugged and looked away, not meeting my eyes.

'I'm sorry we've overstayed our welcome—'

'At least you've finally realised it,' Wayne butted in, before I could finish. 'You've taken advantage for long enough. She was happy to help you out, but it's been over seven months now. You've had ages to find somewhere else. Bet you haven't even bothered looking, have you?'

'I — I may have found somewhere. I'm going to view it tomorrow before work. I'm sorry I've been such a burden to you, Maddie.'

Maddie murmured something but I didn't catch what she said, and Wayne was already pulling her back into the living room, casting a furious glare at Baxter as he went.

Left alone, I realised I was shaking. I would never have believed that Maddie and I would come to this. How on earth had things got so bad between us?

I sank onto the chair and stared at Baxter as he sat, happily looking back at me, as if the whole unpleasant business hadn't touched him at all. I was glad he wasn't afraid or upset. Wayne could be a nasty piece of work, but Baxter didn't seem to let him get to him any more.

I looked at my watch. Jake wouldn't be home from school for another couple of hours. I couldn't face sitting at home with those two until then. Besides, I thought they needed some cooling off space. 'Come on, Baxter. Extra walk for you today.'

Baxter looked delighted at the turn of events. He'd already had a good gallop around the park that morning, tormented Tyson as usual, been treated to a biscuit by Dylan, and been made a huge fuss of by some tiny children and their mothers. The prospect of an unexpected walk was clearly the icing on the cake. I wondered if he considered it a reward for chewing Wayne's jeans. It could be viewed as such, I supposed, and there was a wicked part of me that rather thought he'd earned it.

As we left the house, I decided not to go to the park. I told myself that it had nothing to do with the little voice in my head that whispered it wouldn't be the same without Dylan. It was simply that I fancied a change of scenery. That was all.

After turning right at the top of the street, instead of our usual left, I let Baxter lead the way from that point onwards, not really minding where we walked. I thought about the flat I'd seen advertised. It wasn't very big — just two bedrooms, a small kitchen, bathroom, and lounge — but it looked clean. At least, it had in the photos. What it would look like in real life was another matter.

The landlady had sounded quite pleasant, and she hadn't minded about Jake. I'd been shocked to discover how many properties had strict "no children" rules. It was a first floor flat, which wasn't ideal, and there was no garden, which was a shame. At least it was in a pleasant area of the town, and not too far from the park. I could still take Jake most days, either before or after school, and at weekends.

I wondered if Maddie and I would ever be able to repair our relationship after we left. Would Maddie allow me to take Baxter for his daily walk, or would she not want me and Jake anywhere near her house again? It would break Jake's heart if he didn't see the dog after we moved. He'd grown extremely attached to him.

He'd also grown attached to Dylan. As well as our regular Sunday mornings, we met up with him two or three mornings a week before school and walked the dogs together. Sometimes, we'd only managed half an hour before Dylan had to rush off to work, but he always turned up when he said he would, and Jake was really starting to believe in him. I was really starting to believe in him, too. I tried not to think about what would happen if we couldn't continue our walks with Baxter. Would Dylan still be interested? What excuse would I have to carry on our meetings? I knew Jake would miss him — maybe as much as I would.

A sudden tugging at the lead shook me from my reveries, and I looked around in surprise. Where on earth had Baxter taken us? I didn't recognise it at all.

I sought out the nearest street sign. Glamis Avenue. That rang a bell. I had a vague notion of where we were at least. It was a lovely little street, full of large, detached bungalows and leafy gardens, neat hedges, and wide grass verges. Very pretty. The sort of street I'd always dreamed of living in, where I'd be happy to raise Jake. The sort of street that was way out of my league. I may as well have lusted after a house in Beverley Hills.

Baxter pulled again and I tugged back. 'Behave, Baxter. What on earth's got into you? Walk nicely.'

Baxter appeared oblivious to either my voice or my hand on the lead. He suddenly came to a dramatic halt, almost causing me to trip over him. 'For goodness' sake, Baxter! What are you doing?'

Baxter shot forward, yanking me with him. Frantically, I tightened my grip on the lead and tried to slow him down, but it was like trying to stop a runaway train. He hurtled along the pavement, and I puffed along behind him, wondering what had caught his attention that was so important it made him behave so badly.

Suddenly he stopped dead. Fortunately, I just managed to avoid colliding with him. Standing in front of a garden gate, he stared straight ahead of him. I followed his gaze and froze.

Sitting on the front step of the pretty whitewashed bungalow was a beautiful cat. It had thick, cream fur, a pale grey face, ears and paws, and big blue eyes. It was quite stunning, and it gave the impression that it was all too aware of that fact, as it sat in the weak November sunshine, blinking lazily occasionally, and not appearing in any way concerned that a huge, drooling Boxer dog stood only yards from it, eyeballing it in an alarming manner. Nervously, I wound the lead round my wrist. If Baxter somehow managed to get into the garden, the cat would be history. He was panting quite frantically, every muscle straining, as he pushed his nose through the wrought iron gate and glared at the cat.

I grabbed hold of his collar with my other hand and tried to pull him away, but he wasn't budging. Every time I managed to move him a few inches, he fought against me and moved back. The cat didn't help matters either. It yawned and blinked at him quite provocatively, then stood up, arching its back, as if stretching after a long sleep.

Baxter growled. The cat padded leisurely around the garden, quite obviously aware that Baxter was tracking its every move. It was tormenting him, no doubt about it. I cursed it under my breath. It would soon get a shifty on if I lost my grip on the lead.

I peered through the windows of the bungalow, hoping to catch a glimpse of someone moving around. If I could attract their attention, they could have rushed out and rescued the cat, and Baxter would be persuaded to leave. A van was parked in the drive, so I knew someone was in. It was a bright pink van with the words "Nailed It! Manicures and Acrylics" painted on the sides.

Baxter growled again, and the cat stood still and stared at him. It was too much for Baxter, who hurled himself at the gate. The cat shot under the van and lay there, peering out at the trembling dog with huge blue eyes. I hauled with all my strength on the lead and had just managed to pull Baxter's head out of the gap in the gate, when I heard a woman's voice calling from the back of the bungalow.

'Cupcake! Where are you, Cupcake? Dinner time, darling!'

The cat shot out from under the van and, before Baxter had time to react, it had leapt to the top of the tall gate at the side of the bungalow and disappeared into the back garden. I breathed a huge sigh of relief as Baxter visibly deflated and turned to follow me. His head hung low, and he looked utterly miserable.

'Sorry, Baxter, but there's no way I could let you get hold of that cat. I know it was teasing you but, believe me, it would have been a disaster if I'd let go of your lead, and you're in enough trouble, don't you think?'

Baxter gave a big sigh, and I looked at him, worried. He looked suddenly awfully depressed. Did dogs get depressed? Did he know he was in the way at home and that he was skating on very thin ice? If so, he must have been feeling as uncertain and unwanted as I was.

'What a pair we make, eh, Boy?' I leaned forward, patting him on the back as he padded despondently towards home. Home. Would Maddie's place be his home for much longer? Would it be mine and Jake's home for much longer? What was going to become of us all?

Chapter 7
Moving Day

It was almost as if Baxter knew. I managed to mop the puddle up from the kitchen floor just in time.

Maddie appeared, yawning, just as I put the mop and bucket back in the cupboard.

'Cup of tea, Ellie?'

Maddie had been a lot more pleasant to me since I'd announced that Jake and I would be moving out. The flat wasn't perfect, but over time I could decorate it the way I wanted, and with Jake's and my things out of storage at last, it would soon feel like home.

Jake was upset about the move. I'd taken him to view the flat after I'd signed the tenancy agreement and handed over the deposit, and he'd looked around, obviously not impressed.

'Try to imagine it with our things in it,' I'd urged him. 'Think about your bedroom decorated nicely, and all your posters on the wall, and your books and toys around you. You'll have your own bed again, Jakey! It will be lovely when we've finished.'

He nodded, trying to be noble about the whole thing, probably for my sake. I wanted to put my arms around him and sob. It wasn't what I'd planned for him, but we had to make the best of things. There was no alternative.

'The park's only ten minutes away,' I'd told him. 'We can go there every day if you like.'

'What about Baxter?'

'What about him?'

'Can we still take him to the park? Will we still meet Dylan every day?'

I'd swallowed. 'I — I'm not sure yet. I'll have to ask Maddie. I can't see it being a problem though. She doesn't like walking him does she? I should think she'll be relieved if we carry on walking him for her.'

Jake seemed to cheer up a bit after that. As Maddie popped teabags in two mugs and whistled cheerfully to herself, I decided it was time to make certain of the situation.

'Maddie, about Baxter.'

Maddie stopped whistling. She went to the fridge and took out some milk. 'What about him?' she said eventually. 'If you're going to give me a lecture about taking him for walks and cleaning his teeth and feeding him on time, don't bother. I'm not six years old, you know. I'm a responsible adult. Just because you took over everything, doesn't mean I'm not capable.'

'I wasn't going to say that,' I protested, although privately I had wondered. 'I was simply going to ask you if it would be all right for me and Jake to still take him for walks. It's not that I don't trust you to do it,' I said quickly, seeing Maddie's face. 'It's just that it really cheers Jake up. He loves Baxter so much, and he's been through such a lot already this year. I don't want to take that bit of pleasure away from him.'

Maddie's face softened. 'Of course. That's fine, Ellie. Take him for walks any time you like. Baxter's fond of Jakey, anyone can see that. I wouldn't want to split them up.'

She handed me a mug of tea and took a sip of her own drink. 'So, this flat. It's okay?'

Frankly, I thought it was a bit late to be asking me that. We were moving in that very day, and Maddie hadn't so much as enquired where it was in the two weeks we'd been packing and preparing. It was as if she hadn't even known we were leaving.

Baxter knew, though, I was certain of it. He'd been watching us quite anxiously for days and stuck to our sides like glue. The puddle he'd left that morning only served to confirm my suspicions. He'd never had an accident in the house before. Thank goodness Maddie hadn't seen it.

'It's not too bad.' I shrugged. 'Best of a bad bunch, really. I can make it nicer, though. A lick of paint will cheer it up, and once we get all our furniture in there I'm sure it will be all right.'

Maddie nodded. 'I'm sorry the way things have been,' she said eventually. 'You must think I'm a total bitch.'

I bit my lip, wondering if I should answer honestly

or not.

'Thing is,' said Maddie, fortunately not waiting for a reply, 'Wayne kept going on at me. He wanted you out, and I have an awful feeling he wants to move in.'

'And you don't want him to?'

Maddie hesitated. 'Wayne's all right,' she said eventually, 'but I'm not sure I could stand him actually living here. It can be a bit much sometimes.' She peered at me over her mug and grinned. 'Let's just say I'm often glad when it's Sunday evening and I know he's going home.'

'Then don't let him move in with you,' I advised her. 'If you feel like that now it will only get worse. You strike me as the sort of person who needs her own space. Learn your lesson. No more waifs and strays.'

Maddie's eyes filled with tears. 'I'm sorry, Ellie. I didn't mean to give you such a hard time.'

Despite myself, I put down my mug and went over to my cousin, putting my arm around her. 'It's okay. It's hard living with other people. It was good of you to take us in. You put a roof over our heads for over eight months and that means a lot. Thank you. I hope we can go back to being friends again now I'm out from under your feet.'

Maddie sniffed and nodded. 'I hope so, too. Do you need any help today? I can put work on hold. It wouldn't be a problem.'

I smiled. 'If you're sure? You could always load up the car and take Jake's things to the flat if you don't mind?'

'No problem. I'd like to see where you're going to be living anyway.'

***

Maddie looked around and obviously tried to sound positive. 'Well, it's lovely and cosy,' she said, a bit too brightly.

'You'll be saying that it's compact and bijou next,' I said wryly. 'I know it's small, but there are only the two of us. It'll be fine.'

Maddie nodded. 'I've got some paint in the shed,' she said. 'It's a nice warm cream colour. It will brighten up this room nicely if you'd like it?'

'That would be brilliant. Thanks, Maddie.' I'd wondered how I was going to find the spare money for paint, so her offer was very welcome. Now, the living room was painted dark red, which made it seem even smaller, and very gloomy.

'I'll drop it round for you tomorrow. What time are you at work?'

'Tomorrow? I'm on afternoons. You're sure you don't mind having Jake if I'm asked to do evenings?'

'Told you, not a problem.' Maddie had been falling over herself all day to make amends for her behaviour. I couldn't help feeling relieved. We'd been friends all our lives and I was glad our relationship could still be saved, despite the tensions of the last few months.

Plus, I really needed Maddie's help. It was good to have someone not too far away on call, in case Jake needed picking up from school, or I had to work an evening shift.

Liam was worse than useless in that respect, only willing to bother with his son on alternative Sundays. Any requests for extra help with childcare were met with whining excuses.

The removal van had dropped off the bits of furniture that had been in storage ever since Liam and I had given up our rented house and moved in with his mother. It felt strange seeing them again. I couldn't help remembering the last time I'd seen them, and Maddie seemed to sense what was on my mind.

'Still hurts?' she asked gently. 'Stupid question. This must be so tough for you.'

'Not as tough as it was,' I admitted. 'Did I tell you they've set the date? Apparently, they're getting married in three weeks.'

'No way! That was fast work! Well, it won't last five minutes,' predicted Maddie confidently. 'God, he didn't waste much time did he? When did he tell you?'

'He didn't exactly,' I said.

I told Maddie about the bombshell Jake had dropped on me last Sunday, when he'd excitedly informed me that he was going to have a new brother or sister, and his father was taking him into town the following Saturday to get him a suit, as the wedding had been brought forward.

'Oh, hell, and there was I giving you all that grief. I'm so sorry. You must be devastated.'

I shook my head. 'Not really. Not anymore. It hurt me most that Liam wouldn't even consider having more children with me. I really didn't want Jake to be an only child, but he was adamant one was enough. Then again, I get the distinct impression that this child wasn't exactly planned. Oh, it doesn't matter now does it? Liam's in the past. If it wasn't for Jake I wouldn't have anything to do with him. He wasn't what I thought at all.'

'Most men aren't,' said Maddie gloomily. 'Look at Wayne. All macho and tough, yet he spends more time in front of the mirror than anywhere else, wastes a fortune on hair gel and moisturiser, and has a hissy fit over a packet of mints!'

I couldn't help laughing, remembering the throbbing vein in Wayne's forehead.

'I've been meaning to ask you,' said Maddie suddenly. 'Who's Dylan?'

I felt my face burning and knew I was blushing. Damn. 'Why do you ask?'

'I heard Jakey talking to Baxter about meeting Dylan and Tyson in the park. From what he was saying, I'm guessing — I'm hoping — that Tyson is a dog. But who on earth is Dylan?' She peered at me closely. 'You're blushing! Ooh, come on! Spill the beans!'

'He's just a man we met at the park,' I said

defensively. 'He walks his dog there, too, and we sort of chummed up and decided to walk them together. It's company for the dogs!' I protested when Maddie gave me a quizzical look.

'Then why is your face bright red? I think someone's got a bit of a crush on this Dylan.'

'Don't be daft,' I began, then grinned. 'Well, maybe a little bit. He is quite scrummy.'

'Really? Do tell!'

'We're supposed to be unpacking and putting all this stuff away before Jake leaves school,' I reminded her.

'Plenty of time yet, and I'll pick him up in the car. Tell you what, I'll dig out the kettle and make us a cuppa while you put the bedding on yours and Jake's beds, then we'll sit down for ten minutes, and you can tell me all about him.'

***

'He sounds really lovely,' said Maddie, as I finally brought her up to date with the Dylan situation, 'but you left out the most important part.'

'Oh? What's that?'

'Do you fancy him?'

She nudged me in delight, as a familiar burning sensation left me in no doubt that a crimson flush had just spread from my chest to my forehead.

'You do! Look at you blushing again. What does he look like?'

I realised I was smiling and tried, not altogether successfully, to straighten my face. 'Oh, you know. Nice.'

'Nice? What kind of a word is nice? Nice means nothing, at all! Is he short or tall?'

I considered. 'About the same height as Liam, I'd say. Just under six foot?'

'Fat or thin?'

'Neither. Just right. He runs every morning before he meets us for walks, so I suppose he's pretty fit.'

'Ooh, you want him fit.' Maddie giggled. 'Fair or dark?'

'Sort of mid-brown hair, and before you ask, he has grey-green eyes. And a very sexy mouth.'

Maddie gaped at me. 'Boy, you've got it bad! So, how far have things progressed?'

'I've told you. We just walk the dogs, and we sit on the bench and talk while they play, and Jake goes on the swings. Sometimes, on Sundays, we feed the ducks and get a hot chocolate. It's no big deal.'

'But it is a big deal! It's obvious that he matters to you. Haven't you met him outside of the park?'

I shook my head.

'Why ever not? Haven't you suggested it?'

'It's not like that!' I didn't know how to explain. 'He's never suggested it either. Nothing's happened. We just chat.'

'What do you chat about?'

I thought it wise not to mention all the

conversations Dylan and I had had about Maddie's unwelcoming attitude, and how appalling Wayne was. 'About Liam and what went wrong there, about my job, about the flat. Just stuff.'

'And what about him? What does he talk about? Or is this a one-way conversation?'

'I don't know. Just stuff.' I tried to remember the bits he'd told me. 'He doesn't like football, but he loves rugby. His favourite colour's purple. He hasn't got a sweet tooth, but he's secretly addicted to crisps — especially salt and vinegar ones. He reads thrillers. His favourite author's Phil Rickman—'

'He reads? Wow! I don't think Wayne's read a book since he left school.'

I could well believe that. 'He loves Queen, and he's a world-class air guitar player, apparently.'

She wrinkled her nose. 'Aren't they all? What is it with men and air guitar? Honestly. What does he do for a living?'

'He's an electrician,' I said. 'Has his own business.'

'Well, that's good news,' said Maddie. 'At least he's solvent. Where does he live?'

I realised I hadn't a clue. 'I don't know.' I'd asked, once or twice, but he'd been surprisingly vague, thinking about it. Why was that? 'I should think he doesn't live far from here. After all, he goes to the park pretty frequently.'

'Has he ever been married? Any kids?'

At least I could answer that with confidence. 'No.

Definitely not.'

'Brilliant! So, no baggage.'

'He doesn't believe in marriage,' I admitted, suddenly deflated. 'And he says he's not responsible enough to have kids.'

Maddie looked disappointed. 'Oh. Not so good.' Then she brightened. 'Still, at least he's honest, and that counts for a lot. He's probably just not met the right woman before now. I reckon things will change once you two get together.'

'But we're not getting together.' I sighed. 'We just walk our dogs together. There's been no suggestion of anything else.'

'What, none? No lingering looks, no touchy-feely?'

'Not really.' Although, there had been moments… Times when I'd thought something could have happened, was about to happen, but they always came to nothing. Surely, if Dylan was interested in me, he'd have done something about it by now?

'Maybe he's thinking the same about you,' said Maddie when I voiced my opinion. 'One of you has got to stop being so polite and make a move, and it may just as well be you. Go for it! These are exciting times! A new home, and maybe a new man. Time to put the past behind you, Ellie. Leave Liam behind and move on.'

I looked around the living room and tried to visualise it painted cream and adorned with the photographs, pictures, and ornaments that had been packed away for so long. I could make it into some sort of a home, I knew I could. It would take a bit of money and a lot of effort, and it wouldn't be the kind of home I'd hoped for, but eventually Jake and I would settle, and life would take on a new normality.

A new home had been my main concern for so many months, yet having it at last, making it comfortable didn't seem like such a challenge after all. But a new man? That would take a bit more courage, and I wasn't sure I had enough for the task.

Chapter 8
True to Form

'So, you're settling in all right?' Dylan handed Jake his cookie money, ruffled his hair, and warned him to come straight back, then he turned back to me. 'The flat's okay? No horrific discoveries?'

I laughed. 'Like what?'

'You know. Mice, mould in the bathroom, a creepy neighbour?'

I scooped Tyson onto my knee and re-tied the ribbon, which was coming loose, on the top of the little dog's head. 'Thankfully, no. Haven't even seen the neighbours, the flat is totally mould free and, please, God, we don't have mice. I don't think I'd still be living there if we did.'

'That's a relief,' he said, patting a panting Baxter. 'I was worried.'

'Were you?' My stomach fluttered. It was the perfect moment to say something, put the question to him at last. Were we moving towards something? Was this relationship going anywhere? Or were we just friends who walked their dogs together in the park most days?

'Of course. Jake wasn't happy about leaving

Maddie's was he? And he's already been through so much. I'd hate to think he'd be unhappy, living in some dingy flat somewhere. I'm glad it's decent.'

'Oh. Oh, yes, no need to worry.'

I tried hard to sound positive, though the disappointment was seeping its way through my bones. I should have asked, but I couldn't make myself do it. He'd never given me any clue that he was interested in me romantically, and if I said something, I may have just embarrassed him, scared him off. I may never see him again, and I didn't think I could bear that.

But, just sometimes, he would look at me with an expression in those lovely grey green eyes that quite took my breath away. At moments like that, I could almost imagine that he had feelings for me. But it wasn't worth the risk. It could all be wishful thinking. He'd said nothing and until he did…

'I've just painted the living room. Maddie gave me some cream paint, and it looks much brighter now.'

'Maddie gave you the paint? Wow! That was good of her.' He pushed Baxter's paws off his knee and scolded him gently when he tried to jump up again.

I smiled at his sarcastic tone. 'Actually, she's been lovely since we moved out. Quite her old self. She even came around and helped me paint. Things are practically the same between us as they used to be.'

'That's good. You've forgiven her then?'

'Forgiven her? For what?'

'For making you feel so unwelcome.'

I shrugged. 'She was struggling. Wayne was making demands on her and putting pressure on her to evict us and, besides, she's used to living alone. It was tough having me and Jake there, invading her space. I can't forget that she put over a roof over our heads when we needed it most. I'll always be grateful for that. I don't know what we'd have done without her. There's nothing to forgive.'

'You're a very special person, Ellie,' he said softly.

'Me? Nothing special about me.'

I re-tied Tyson's ribbon for the second time, though it didn't need it.

'But there is. You're so forgiving. Not just of Maddie, but of Liam. After everything he put you through, you still encourage him to see his son, and I've never once heard you bad mouth him to Jakey.'

I stared at him. 'Of course not! Liam's his father. Jake doesn't need to hear any negative stuff about his dad. He's been through enough. I'm trying to keep everything as painless and smooth as I can for him. Any mother would do the same.'

He shook his head. 'No, they wouldn't, Ellie. Believe me.'

'I'm sorry. I forgot.' He looked so sad for a moment that I longed to reach out and touch his face and I had to force myself not to.

'So,' I said brightly, 'it's the carol concert on Saturday. Is your niece taking part?'

'What?' He looked baffled at my sudden change of

subject for a moment then smiled. 'Oh, yes. I think her class are singing Away in a Manger. At least, that's my best guess, from her endless warbling every time I see her.'

'Oh, bless her. Are you going?'

Dylan shook his head. 'Sadly, the school's limited tickets to two per child, due to high demand, unbelievably. I was gutted, obviously. Still, I'm sure Greg and Colleen will enjoy themselves. You'll be going, I guess?'

'Of course.'

'Won't it be awkward? With Liam there, I mean.'

'We're adults. We'll just have to put up with it. At least Luscious Laura won't be there. As you say, the school limited tickets to two per child, which meant there wasn't a spare one for her, thank God. She wasn't very happy about that I can tell you. Liam wasn't too thrilled, either.'

'I'm surprised she wanted to go to a school carol concert, to be honest. Doesn't sound like her sort of thing, from what you've said.'

'I suspect it's more that she didn't want Liam and me alone together. Well, alone with a few hundred other people, obviously. Anyway, she's going to have to get used to doing school stuff now.'

'Oh?'

I hesitated, but there seemed no reason not to confide in him. 'She's pregnant. They're bringing the wedding forward, for obvious reasons.'

'Oh, Ellie. I'm sorry.'

'Don't be. Honestly, I'm fine. So long as Liam doesn't push Jake further out of his life to make room for the new baby, it really doesn't matter.'

'I'm sure that won't happen. He's going to the concert isn't he? That must mean he really wants to spend time with Jake. He didn't have to do it, after all. Good sign, huh?'

'Yes, absolutely.'

He smiled, then reached into the backpack that he'd put on the ground, and as Jake came back he handed him a carrier bag.

'Here you go, Jakey. You've probably got one already, but I just saw them in the shop and thought... Well, you can never have too much chocolate can you?'

Jake beamed on opening the bag. 'An advent calendar! Wow, it really is nearly Christmas. I haven't got one yet, have I, Mum?'

'No,' I admitted. 'I meant to get you one, but it kept slipping my mind. Thanks, Dylan. That's so kind of you.'

He shrugged, embarrassed. 'It's just a calendar. No big deal.'

I put Tyson down. 'Shall we let these two go for a run now?' I asked, standing. 'I could do to stretch my legs actually.'

'Sure,' Dylan agreed. 'I know Jake may be exhausted after his exertions on Saturday evening,' he said with a wink, 'but do you still want to meet up here on the

Sunday morning before he goes to his dad's?'

I smiled. 'I'd love to.' It felt like he'd offered me the world. I stood up but pulled a face when my mobile rang.

'Just a moment.' I noted, with dread, the name on the screen. What did Liam want? I wandered a little away from Dylan and Jake and answered the call. 'Liam? What can I do for you?'

'Ellie, I'm really sorry but I won't be able to go to the carol concert on Saturday.'

'You've got to be kidding me! Why not?'

'It really can't be helped. Laura's gran wants to meet me. She can't travel down here, so we're going up to Scotland to stay with her, and we won't be back until the Saturday night. I feel awful about it, but what can I do? Jakey won't mind will he?'

'He won't have to will he?' I snapped. 'Can't you come back a bit earlier?'

'It's a long drive from Scotland. I'll be knackered. I can't make a promise I can't keep,' he said, with no apparent trace of irony, 'and I really don't think I'll be there, so it's best I tell you now isn't it? Be reasonable. Anyway, I must go. Tell Jake I really am sorry, and I hope the concert goes brilliantly.'

'What about the day after? If you've been driving the day before will you be up to having Jakey at yours? I don't want him all packed and ready to go, and then you cancel on him at the last minute.'

'Oh, no, I should think that will be fine. I'll let you

know if not. Bye, Ellie.'

I ended the call and shoved the phone back in my coat pocket, all too aware that I'd have to break the news to Jake that his father wouldn't be in the audience on Saturday night after all. So much for Liam spending extra time with him. I should have known it was too good to be true.

'Problem?' Dylan looked at me curiously, but I shook my head. There was no reason to spoil Jake's morning. He loved our trips to the park with Baxter, Dylan, and Tyson. I would break it to him gently when we got home.

Chapter 9
Hark, the Herald Angels Sing!

The school hall was packed. Gaudy red and gold streamers were draped around the room, and a rather impressive Christmas tree stood in the far corner, wearing decorations that had probably been around since Dylan had attended the school.

Every wall bore paintings done by the children, demonstrating what Christmas meant to them. For every Nativity scene, there were around twenty Father Christmases, and a fair few Rudolphs, which pretty much proved what their priorities were.

Hundreds of parents were crammed into tiny plastic chairs, reminiscing about their own school days, and muttering about needing a cigarette. Members of staff strutted around, trying to look important, and the gloriously named Cottesmore Primary Orchestra — which consisted of around twenty kids playing various instruments, conducted by a wild-haired teacher who already looked in need of Prozac — tuned up.

I flicked through the programme, sighing inwardly as I realised how long the evening was likely to go on for. I tried to ignore the sadness on noticing how many parents were in couples. I had no one to talk to about Jake. No one to whisper excitedly to, no one to remind to get the camera out the minute he appeared on stage, no one to voice my worries to that he'd suffer stage fright or forget the words to his class's carols.

'Ellie?'

I looked up and blushed when I saw Dylan standing there, looking down at me. He looked quite gorgeous in black jeans, with a grey sweater under his leather jacket. He stood hand-in-hand with a cute little blonde girl, who eyed me curiously.

'Are you alone? Is Liam late?'

I sighed and shook my head. 'Liam couldn't make it after all, so here I am, all alone.'

'Ah.' He gave me a sympathetic look. 'Sorry to hear that.'

'Yeah, well, there you go. Seems Laura's grandmother felt a desperate need to meet Liam, so they've gone to visit her. Who's this little poppet?'

'My niece, Lucy.' Dylan smiled down at the little girl, who beamed back at him. 'Greg has to work late, and her mum had a bit of an accident yesterday, so guess who got roped in to come to the carol concert with her?'

'Oh, no, I'm sorry to hear that. Is your mummy okay?' I asked.

'Mummy hurt her foot.' said Lucy solemnly. 'It's gone all blue and fat. She can't get her shoe on any more.'

'Oh, dear.'

'Daddy says it's her own fault,' the child informed me.

I bit my lip, trying not to smile. 'Well, I hope she gets better soon.'

'She can't walk properly, and she keeps pulling faces and saying ow and swearing a lot.'

'All right, Lucy. We don't need the details,' Dylan said with a sigh.

'She's a real cutie,' I whispered. 'What happened to her mum?'

'Colleen wanted to get the Christmas tree out of the loft,' he murmured. 'Greg told her to wait 'til he got home that evening, and he'd do it, while she held the ladder, but she decided to go ahead anyway. To make matters worse, she didn't even get the stepladder but just balanced on a chair. Stupid. I mean, I love Coll, but honestly, it could have been serious. Still, on a positive note, I don't think she'll try that again.'

He smiled suddenly and waved, and my heart leapt at Jake heading towards us.

'Okay, mate?' Dylan said, ruffling his hair. 'Are we doing this thing then?'

'What are you doing here?' Jake's face lit up. 'Brilliant. Who's this?'

He looked suspiciously at the little girl, who was suddenly clinging possessively to her uncle.

'This is my niece, Lucy. She's in Miss Rawson's class.'

'Oh, she's one of the babies,' said Jake dismissively. 'They're only doing one song. I'm doing two, aren't I, Mum?'

'You certainly are,' I said, rolling my eyes at Dylan. 'Can't wait.'

Dylan winked at me, and my tummy fluttered in a very teenage crush fashion. I hadn't felt like that for such a long time — not since I'd first met Liam, in fact. Maybe not even then.

'Right, well, I have to get this one backstage,' Dylan said, looking down at Lucy. 'Coming with me, mate?' he asked Jake. 'You don't want to be late, do you?'

Jake agreed that he didn't and took hold of Dylan's other hand, which caused Lucy to give him a look that would have flayed anyone with less courage.

'So, I take it that seat's going spare?' murmured Dylan, nodding at the empty chair beside me that Liam's behind wouldn't be filling.

'It is,' I confirmed. 'Do you want it?'

'If that's okay with you,' he said, and I smiled.

As I watched him taking Jake and Lucy to their class teachers, I decided his behind was rather more pleasant to view than Liam's anyway, and that I'd be quite thrilled to have it plonked beside me while I sat through two hours of badly sung Christmas carols and a few horrific recorder recitals.

It had to be said, sitting beside Dylan had a positive effect on me. For the first time I began to get in the mood for Christmas. As we listened to a sweet little cherub with no front teeth warbling The First Noel, I got quite teary.

Dylan handed me a tissue. 'Coll warned me that Christmas carols and children are a potent mix,' he whispered. 'She said I'd cry and handed me several tissues, just in case.'

'You're not crying though,' I replied, dabbing my eyes. 'It's just me, being pathetic.'

'Is it because Liam's let you down?' he asked sympathetically. 'Or is it just the whole divorce thing and the situation with Laura? It must be even tougher at Christmas.'

I shook my head. I didn't, for one minute, want him to think I was pining for my ex-husband. 'It's not that. I just suddenly found my Christmas spirit. It's been sadly lacking so far this year.'

'Probably the job you do,' he said. 'I mean, supermarkets ram Christmas down your throat from September. Even I get sick to death of hearing Slade when I do my shopping once a week. Having to work in it must drive you insane. Which supermarket do you work in, by the way?'

'Maister's. Do you ever shop there?'

'Sometimes. It's quite upmarket isn't it?' He grinned at me. 'Bit too posh for the likes of me.'

'It's not the cheapest supermarket there is,' I admitted. 'I wouldn't shop there if I didn't work there, but I do get a discount, so it's worth it for some stuff.'

'Are you working tomorrow?'

'No. They're pretty good there and try to work around Jake. I rarely work weekends. Sometimes I work on the Sundays he visits Liam, but they mostly fit my shifts in with school hours. Kylie, who does the rota, has kids herself and is really understanding. I can't complain.'

We clapped loudly as the cherub finished her song, and there was a general shuffling and yawning in the hall while we all waited for the next act.

'What about you?'

'What about me?'

'You said you were an electrician. Do you work for a company, or for yourself?'

'Myself. I used to work for Claxton's, but then I thought, why am I working to make them richer? It seemed a better idea to work for myself. Not as simple as that as it turned out, and it took me a few years to build up the business, but it's doing okay now. I manage to pay the mortgage and the bills, and I have a bit left over at the end of the month, so I guess I can't complain either.'

'We're very easily pleased,' I said, smiling.

'It seems so. Although, I think I'm getting a lot choosier as I get older.'

'Oh?'

He wasn't smiling. In fact, he looked quite pensive. I wondered what he was thinking, but before I could press him the curtains opened again, and the nursery class was ushered on stage.

'Oh, it's Lucy's lot,' Dylan whispered, rolling his eyes. 'Prepare to be dazzled.'

But as the class of three and four-year-olds made their wobbly way through Away in a Manger, it was Dylan who seemed dazzled. I watched, feeling quite emotional, as he swallowed down the lump in his throat and blinked away tears. When the carol ended and the class took a bow, he was the first on his feet, clapping furiously.

'God,' he admitted, sinking back into his chair, and shaking his head, 'I had no idea. How do they do that? Grab you like that I mean?'

I patted his hand. 'That's children and Christmas carols. As Colleen said, it's a potent mix.'

'I guess so. Wow.' He looked at me sheepishly. 'Sorry.'

'Don't be daft,' I said. 'I think it's lovely.'

'Do you?' His eyes held mine, and it was my turn to swallow down the lump in my throat.

'Jake's class,' I murmured.

'What?'

'It's Jake's class.'

I'd heard the orchestra start the introduction to Hark! The Herald Angels Sing and knew it was my son's turn to dazzle without even glancing at the stage.

'Oh, right. Yes, of course. Great stuff.'

We both settled in our seats and stared fixedly at the front where Jake's class had assembled and were looking increasingly nervous.

'Go on, Jakey. You can do it,' I whispered, and shivered as Dylan took hold of my hand and squeezed it.

The class sang my favourite carol beautifully, if I say so myself, and tears ran down my cheeks as their voices soared in chorus. Beside me, Dylan silently urged Jake on, and his hand stayed firmly in mine throughout. It was a few moments of pure bliss, only broken when the carol ended and Dylan dropped my hand as we all clapped, and Jake left the stage.

Finally, after almost two hours, the concert ended, with the entire school gathered on stage to sing We Wish You a Merry Christmas. We all clapped and cheered, the curtains closed, and we were free. Except, I felt suddenly dismayed that it was all over. So much so, I was quite relieved when the head teacher appeared from behind the curtain and, after thanking us all for coming, announced that drinks and refreshments were available in the canteen.

And as all proceeds would go towards the school funds, it made it impossible for anyone to refuse to buy some. Didn't it? Well, Dylan seemed to agree at any rate, and as soon as Lucy and Jake arrived at our side we all headed off to the canteen, where willing volunteers had lined up behind tables of hot and cold drinks and trays of mince pies.

'Orange juice!' squealed Lucy. 'Can I have one, Uncle Dylan?'

'Of course. Jakey, do you want one, too?'

'Yes, please, Dylan,' said Jake.

'Ellie? Orange juice, tea, or coffee?'

'Tea, please.' I took the plastic cup from his hand, hoping he wouldn't notice that mine was trembling, and sipped nervously at the hot, weak liquid. Lucy and Jake sat at a table, along with several other children, and discussed their outstanding performances. Parents milled around, drinking, eating, and generally agreeing that their children had been absolute stars.

Dylan finished his drink and took our empty plastic cups back to the table. I sank onto a chair at the edge of the room and watched him as he made easy conversation with the teachers who were pouring the drinks.

He drew a few admiring glances from some of the women who stood nearby, and I fought down a pang of jealousy. Honestly, what was wrong with me! He didn't belong to me, and I had no right to feel jealous. He turned his head and gave me a beautiful smile. My stomach flipped over, my lips instantly curving and smiling back.

For a moment we gazed at each other, and the crowds around us faded into the background until there was just the two of us, and I knew in that moment that I was lost.

Slipping out of the room took me into an empty corridor, and I stood with my back against the wall, waiting. The door opened and he walked slowly over to me, saying nothing for a moment. Nervously, I plucked at a button on my coat, pulling an imaginary thread. Then my hand stilled as his own rested upon it. I froze, my heart pounding with excitement and nerves. Slowly, I lifted my gaze to meet his and saw the same emotions reflected in those grey-green eyes. His fingers softly stroked mine and then his hand cupped my hand and he squeezed it gently. I squeezed back and had to suppress the desire to leap upon him as his eyes burned into mine.

Then his gaze dropped to my mouth. He edged closer, his breath hot on my cheek. My eyes closed. He was going to kiss me. I could almost feel the brush of his lips on my skin. I swore I could hear those herald angels singing.

The door opened with a bang.

'Are we going home now?'

My eyes flew open in shock and Dylan leapt back as if he'd been burnt.

'Sorry, Lucy. Yes, if you're ready. Where's Jake?'

Jake sauntered out of the room, looking fed up. 'She wants to go home. Are we going home too, Mum?'

'Well, er, I don't see why not.'

I looked at Dylan.

Obviously embarrassed, he cleared his throat. 'You don't drive, do you? Do you, er, need a lift or anything?'

'No, it's fine. It's not far. We can walk,' I assured him.

'You're sure?' His eyes searched mine. 'I really don't mind.'

I smiled. 'Honestly. It's okay. Come on, I'll walk with you as far as the car park anyway.'

We headed out into the cold, December evening air, and I watched, my heart aching, as Dylan scooped a clearly exhausted Lucy into his arms and carried her across the playground.

'Why is she yawning?' demanded Jake. 'It's only eight o'clock.'

'All right, Jakey. Just remember, she's a lot younger than you,' I rebuked him gently.

'Can't you remember what it was like when you were four?' said Dylan.

'Dad lived with us then,' said Jake. 'We had a house of our own, but then we had to go and live with Grandma. I don't know why. But Grandma didn't really want us there, and I didn't like it anyway.'

'I'm sure your grandmother was pleased to have you,' said Dylan.

'She wasn't, was she, Mum?' said Jake. 'I don't care anyway. She smelled funny and she made me eat broccoli. I don't like broccoli.'

'I don't like broccoli either,' said Lucy, with some feeling. 'It's yuk.'

'Yeah, it is,' said Jake. 'Who wants little trees on their plate?'

Lucy giggled. 'They *are* little trees! I said they were, but Mummy said they weren't.'

'Well, they are. You were right,' said Jake, looking up at her as she peered at him from over Dylan's shoulder. He fell in step beside them. 'Where do you live? Does your dad live with you?'

'Of course he does,' said Lucy, sounding surprised. 'I live in a nice house, and Daddy says we've got the smartest garden in the street, doesn't he, Uncle Dylan?'

'Yes, he does. Frequently.' He grinned at me. 'Seems like they've decided they quite like each other, after all,' he murmured.

He reached in his pocket and drew out his car keys, rattling them in his hand. He could have held my hand instead, but it seemed the moment had passed. I wondered if he was regretting his actions. The thought scared me. Had it all been a horrible mistake on his part?

'I'm not tired at all,' Jake announced, taking my hand. 'But I'm a lot bigger than Lucy. You'll be home soon,' he told her. 'Don't worry.'

We headed to the car park in silence. I had no idea what to say. What had just happened? Had I been imagining things? Had Dylan really been about to kiss me or was it all in my head? He still hadn't said anything, and that left me totally confused. I was about to say goodbye and head off through the gate when Lucy's excited cry made me look round in surprise.

'Daddy's here! Look, Uncle Dylan! Daddy's here.'

We all looked across to where a man of similar build and colouring to Dylan leaned against a dark estate car. He raised a hand and waved, but his other hand was clutching a lead.

'He must have finished work earlier than expected,' muttered Dylan.

I looked at him in surprise. He didn't seem particularly pleased about it.

'He's brought Tyson,' observed Jake. 'Look, Lucy, Tyson's come to see you.'

'Who's Tyson?' said Lucy, sounding puzzled.

Jake laughed. 'That dog there,' he said, pointing to her father. 'Look, your dad's got him.'

Lucy pulled a face. 'That's not Tyson,' she said scornfully. 'That's Mitzi, Mummy's dog.'

'Mitzi?' I stared at Dylan, who looked mortified. 'Who's Mitzi? What's she talking about? I thought that was Tyson, and I thought she was your dog?'

'Yes, well, I can explain…'

'Can you? Go on then.'

'Daddy!' Lucy struggled in Dylan's arms and, as he put her on the ground, she ran to her father.

The new arrival scooped her up, laughing. 'Hello, angel. How did it go, my clever girl? I'll bet you stole the show.' He nodded at Dylan. 'Thanks for stepping in, bro. You're a star.' He smiled at me, his eyes full of curiosity.

I tried to smile back but couldn't. My stomach was churning. What the hell was going on? Why had Dylan lied about Tyson?

Greg looked uncertainly between us, obviously sensing a problem. 'Er, I finished work earlier than I thought, and I was hoping to catch the end of the concert, but realised I was too late. Still, I'll take her home with me, save you having to come back to ours, eh? Unless you want to, of course. Thanks again, Dylan,' he said, opening the car door and ushering Lucy and Mitzi inside.

We watched them drive off in silence. Jake tugged at my hand.

'Are we going, Mum?'

'Jakey, wait by the gate. I'll catch you up in a moment,' I promised him.

He frowned, looking from me to Dylan and back again. 'Are you all right, Mum?'

'I'm fine. I just want to talk to Dylan about something. I won't be long. Stay by the gate and don't step outside the car park, okay? I won't be a minute.'

Jake hesitated, but he turned and headed over to the gate. I watched, making sure that he wasn't going through it, then turned back to Dylan. 'So, what's going on?'

He ran his hand through his hair, as I'd noticed him do before when he was stressed. 'I know it looks bad, but it really isn't. I just got caught up in something I couldn't get out of. That morning when we first met, remember?'

'Of course I remember.' I would never forget it.

'You sort of assumed that I had a dog, and I — I went along with it. I'd been sounding such a know-all, and I thought you'd think I was an arrogant git, giving you all this advice and not actually owning a dog myself.

'I told you about Tyson because he's one of my mate's dogs. He's a bull terrier, and as macho as they come. Lee only got him a couple of weeks ago from a rescue centre, and I guess he'd stuck in my mind. Then, when you suggested I bring him for a walk with you all, I was kind of stuck. I should have admitted everything then, but I was so embarrassed, and besides, I really wanted to meet up with you all. So I agreed, thinking I could borrow Tyson and bring him with me.

'Trouble was, when I asked my mate, he told me it would never work, because, although Tyson is brilliant with people, he's a nightmare around other dogs. I didn't want him attacking Baxter and causing mayhem in the park, so I had to think of something else. Unfortunately, the only other dog I could think of was Mitzi. I had to throw myself on Coll's mercy and tell her everything. She told me I was an idiot, but she let me borrow the dog, and that's why I was a bit late that first morning, and why I had to make up all that rubbish about Mitzi being gay.'

'Wouldn't it have been easier to just admit the truth?'

'Absolutely one-hundred per cent, yes.' He shook his head. 'I'm a prize idiot and a terrible liar. I really am sorry, Ellie. I found myself panicking when you realised she was a girl, and I just couldn't believe the stuff I was saying.' He took my hand and squeezed it. 'Forgive me?'

I wanted to. Really badly. But the memory of Liam and his endless lies made me reluctant to do so.

'It's just that…' My voice trailed off. How could I explain it? He would never understand.

'It's just that Liam lied to you all the time, and now you're worried that I'm the same.'

So, he did understand, after all. The thought was comforting, but even so…

'Are you?' My voice was little more than a whisper. 'I don't know what's going on between us. Where is this heading?'

Well, at least I'd finally had the guts to ask. I realised I was trembling, and that he was still holding my hand.

He stared at me for a long moment then let it go. 'I'm not Liam, Ellie. Really, I'm not.'

'That doesn't answer my question. In fact, it doesn't answer either of them.'

He stuck his hands in his jacket pockets and looked around helplessly. 'I'd better get home, and you need to take Jake back. It's been a long day for him. Will you still meet me tomorrow morning? We can feed the ducks, and we'll talk.'

'I — I suppose so.'

'Thank you, Ellie.' He looked anxious, and rather sad as he turned away.

I hurried over to the gate and ushered Jake out into the street, desperate to get away and clear my head. I couldn't work out what the hell was going on in Dylan's mind, and why he couldn't give me a straight answer. I supposed he might be able to do so the next morning at the park. I pushed away the thought that it would give him a whole night to come up with some plausible story.

He'd said he wasn't like Liam, and the little voice in my head was urging me to believe him. I wanted so badly to listen to it, but I was in too deep, and I couldn't bear to go through all that again.

Chapter 10
A Question of Trust

I barely slept that night, unlike Jake who slept solidly until almost eight o'clock the following morning.

All alone, I sipped my tea and wondered if I should wake him or leave him for another half hour.

Liam hadn't been in touch. Obviously, they were all home, so Jake would be able to visit. He was usually collected at around ten-thirty, so if we wanted to meet Dylan in the park, we'd have to hurry. I took another gulp of my tea and considered what had happened between me and Dylan. There was no denying the chemistry between the two of us. It wasn't just the school's huge, cast-iron radiators that had made me so hot and bothered in that corridor the night before, and I knew he'd felt the same. If only he hadn't told those stupid lies about Tyson.

Yet did it really matter? When I'd first met Liam, I'd had an uncomfortable feeling about him immediately, and the little voice had been nagging away at me right from the start. I hadn't had that feeling with Dylan. On the contrary, I'd felt safe with him from our first meeting. The little voice had believed he was someone

I could trust. Had I been so wrong about him? I didn't want to be betrayed again, but was telling a few white lies about a dog really the same as the stuff Liam had lied about? Or should I draw a line in the sand right then and say even one lie was one too many, and it was over before it had begun?

Then again, he said he'd wanted to meet up with us, and that was why he'd pretended to have a dog. Didn't that say something? Didn't that tell me that he'd been attracted to me right from the beginning, just as I'd been attracted to him? Didn't that count for anything?

I wished I wasn't at work that afternoon. I thought I had a headache coming on and wasn't in the mood for grouchy customers and miserable colleagues who'd be moaning that they hated working Sundays, especially in the run up to Christmas, when everything was hectic, and people were grumpy, and the queues seemed to stretch forever down the aisles.

Kylie had been deeply apologetic when she'd called earlier that morning. 'I wouldn't ask, Ellie, you know that, but Suzie's rung in sick — probably a hangover to be honest — and Glenda and Jen aren't answering their phones. Not that I can blame them. They've already worked extra shifts this week. I know it's Liam's weekend with Jake, so I was wondering if you could do a few hours this afternoon. I'd really appreciate it.'

I'd hardly been able to say no when Kylie had done me so many favours, but it had just about put the tin hat on a pretty rubbish weekend.

Hearing Jake moving about upstairs, I got up to make his breakfast. Luckily, his bag was already packed. We'd have to be quick if we wanted to go to the park and then get back in time for Liam's arrival. The phone beeped just as I opened the cereal packet, and I froze. No doubt it would be Liam, cancelling Jake's visit. I banged the box of Cheerios on the worktop and snatched up my phone, glaring at the screen and practically daring Liam to have the nerve to disappoint his son yet again.

Except the message wasn't from Liam, and my breath caught as I realised that I'd received my very first message from Dylan. We'd exchanged numbers in case either of us ever needed to cancel or let the other know we were going to be late to the park, but we'd never actually made use of them before.

I trembled, wondering what he was going to say to me. A part of me was bursting with excitement, and I tried to push those feelings down. I was acting like a teenager with a first crush. It was embarrassing. Still, I shook as I tapped the screen, hoping against hope that it was some sort of loving message — some declaration of his feelings for me. My heart sank as I read the text.

✉Really sorry, Ellie. I can't make it today. Something's come up. I promise we'll talk soon. Dylan xx

What had come up? What was so important that

116

he'd cancel the meeting that he seemed so desperate to have with me yesterday? And more importantly, what did those two kisses mean?

I tried to think. One kiss was just being friendly, wasn't it? The sort of thing one'd put on anyone's text. But two meant something quite different. Or was it the other way around? I really couldn't remember and knew I'd drive myself insane thinking about it if I carried on like that, so I pushed all thoughts of Dylan away. For all of five seconds.

'Morning, darling. How are you feeling this morning? Is your throat sore?'

Jake looked puzzled. 'No. Why?'

I smiled. 'Just me then. Must be all the cheering I did last night. Here's your cereal. You've had a nice long sleep. You don't have to hurry, by the way, because we're not going to the park this morning.'

Jake looked bitterly disappointed. 'Why not? What about Baxter?'

'I'll ask Maddie to take him today. Dylan can't make it, so I think I'll have a nice easy morning for a change and chill out before work.'

'Why can't he make it?' demanded Jake, spooning cereal into his mouth.

I pulled a face. 'Don't speak with your mouth full, Jakey. And I have no idea. I didn't ask. It's really none of our business is it?'

'Are you and Dylan arguing?'

I looked at him in surprise. 'Of course not. What

made you say that?'

'You looked very cross yesterday, and you made me go on without you which usually means you want to talk to somebody without my hearing and that usually means a row. Well, it does with Dad anyway, so it probably does with Dylan too.'

'No, no, Jakey,' I protested. 'We didn't row, I promise you. We just have some stuff to sort out, and that has nothing to do with not going to the park this morning.'

'Really?'

'Really. Now, how about we take half an hour and watch some television before we get ready?'

***

'It's only a little white lie, Ellie.' Maddie's eyes were warm with understanding as she put down her coffee and patted my arm. 'I know what you're thinking, but you can't judge all men by Liam.'

We were in The Beehive Café on the high street. It was Wednesday afternoon, and I'd heard nothing from Dylan all week. I'd tried to be philosophical about it, telling myself that he was a busy man, and something must have come up, but I wasn't convinced.

He'd behaved very oddly at the carol concert, and then I'd seen nothing of him since. I couldn't help feeling hurt.

Maddie had popped into Maister's for a few things,

just as I was finishing my shift. It had apparently taken only seconds for her to ascertain that I was feeling low, and she'd suggested we go for a coffee in town. I was too fed up to argue, although I'd promised myself that I'd go straight home and get on with decorating the flat for Christmas.

I'd got our old Christmas tree and decorations, and I was determined to bring some cheer into the place, despite my worries because, quite frankly, I couldn't stand it a moment longer. It was so drab. The whole flat felt drab.

I knew, in my heart of hearts, that no amount of tinsel, or fairy lights, or candles would make it the kind of home I'd wanted for myself and Jake. I missed having a garden, and I knew he did too. I hated the small windows, the cheap carpet, the old-fashioned bathroom suite and the ancient kitchen units.

I hated the gas fire on the wall, and the electric cooker that had seen better days. The thought of spending years living there pulled me down. I couldn't look on the bright side any more. Nothing was right.

Despite my misgivings I'd agreed to go to the café with Maddie. Better to spend an hour or so there in bright, cheerful surroundings than be at home. Left to my own devices I knew I would only brood, and that was the worst thing I could do.

'I reckon it's a good sign anyway.'

My eyes widened. 'How can the fact that he lied to me be a good sign?'

'Well, think about it. He obviously fancied you like mad from the moment he saw you, or why would he make up a dog as an excuse to walk with you every day? He's gone to a whole lot of trouble to spend time with you. I'd be flattered.'

'Would you? I suppose... But then, why did he cancel our meeting the next day? Why haven't I heard a word from him since?'

Maddie considered. 'Maybe he's just embarrassed. He must have felt cornered when his brother turned up with the dog in front of you all and imagine how stupid he felt having to confess the truth. Bet he's worrying himself sick, especially since he knows how you feel about being lied to. Give him the benefit of the doubt.'

I mulled that over. Was Maddie right? Was I making something out of nothing? Maybe there was a reason for Dylan's odd behaviour after all. Maybe he did have a lot of work on, or maybe he really was too embarrassed to meet me. Maybe I should call him. Smooth things over.

I tried to think about something else. 'How are things with you and Wayne? Any progress on the moving in situation?'

Maddie pulled a face. 'He's practically moved all his stuff in without even asking me. I can't move in that bathroom. My God, he's vain! You should see the bottles and cans and jars on the shelves. No room for my products. And it gets worse.'

'Really?' I wasn't sure I wanted to know. How much worse could it be? Maddie took a mouthful of coffee and seemed to consider where her loyalties lay. She apparently decided they didn't lie with Wayne, which I thought wasn't a good omen for their future.

'You know he used to play football for Harpington United?'

'Did he? No, I didn't know.' I was quite surprised. Harpington United were the town's football team, and although they weren't exactly premier league, they were doing quite well, having recently been promoted.

'Not the main team of course. The under twenty-one squad. I'm going back a few years.'

'Aren't you just,' I murmured.

'He could have been as good as Beckham, he says, until a knee injury put paid to his career. Anyway, it turns out that he's got a whole stack of memorabilia from those days. I mean, badges, kit, medals, newspaper cuttings, a signed photo of him getting a hug from the club mascot. Honestly, a whacking great big picture of him and a six-foot badger. Why would anyone want to keep that?'

'A six-foot badger?'

'The club was sponsored by Badger's Jam.'

'Oh, of course.' That made sense, I thought, taking another sip of coffee.

'His prized possession is his scrapbook. He's got everything that was ever printed about his football career in there. Photos, press reports, programmes. It's sickening. The worst of it is, he expects me to put it all on display. He wants to buy a big glass cabinet and stick the whole lot in the living room so that everyone gets to see how wonderful he was.'

'And you're not keen?'

Maddie looked aghast. 'Of course I'm not keen! Would you be? Mind you, there is one benefit to his fanaticism. He's going to have to behave himself for the rest of his life, or else. Any sign of a wandering eye and I'll be making a bonfire of the lot, quicker than you can say matches. And I don't mean football matches.'

'You're evil!' I said, trying not to laugh.

'Yeah, it has been said.' Maddie glanced around. 'Do you fancy another latte?'

I checked my watch, sighing inwardly as the chattering from other customers in the café was drowned out by yet more Christmas music. 'No, I'd better get off. If I hear Wonderful Christmastime once more, I may hurl this cup through the window.'

She winced. 'I know. Everywhere you go, it's the same bloody tunes, over and over. It must drive you mad, working at that supermarket. John Lennon's, War is Over. That's all he knew.'

'I know. Not a cheery thought is it? Although it's better than a lot of the other songs they keep blasting at us all day. Anyway it's not just that, I promise. I have to collect Jakey from school.'

'Do you want a lift?'

'No, it's fine. I can walk there in time. Might do me

good to stretch my legs, get some fresh air. I need to clear my head.'

Maddie winked at me. 'Cheer up, eh? Bet this time next week you'll be laughing at all these doubts and worries you're having.'

'Maybe.' I smiled. 'Thanks for the coffee, Maddie. I really appreciate it.'

'No problem. I'm glad to get out of the house for a bit, truth to tell. Working from home has its good points, obviously, but sometimes I feel I can go a bit stir crazy.'

'I'll pop round in the morning and take Baxter for a walk. How's he doing?'

'Missing you and Jake. He's pining, and nothing I do or say is cheering him up,' Maddie confessed. 'It's a shame you couldn't have him in that flat. He much prefers your company to mine.'

'Wayne's okay with him?'

'I think they've come to a mutual agreement. They basically ignore each other entirely. It's like they refuse to acknowledge the other's existence. It's almost funny.'

I laughed. 'Sounds like you've got quite a lot to deal with yourself. I'll be round about nine, after I drop Jake off at school. I'll take him out on Saturday, too. I promised Jake that we could go back to the park, though I can't say I'm looking forward to that.'

'It will all come right in the end, Ellie. Promise.' Maddie scooped up her handbag and hugged me. 'See you tomorrow morning. Give my love to Jakey.'

We parted outside The Beehive Café, and I turned and headed in the direction of Jake's school. I wondered if he'd like to help with decorating the tree when we got home. It would give us both something to do, at any rate, and was better than staring at the television all evening. I nipped into the discount shop and bought some Christmas cards. I'd give some to Jake, and he could send them to his friends at school. The teacher had provided a post box for the classroom, and encouraged all the children to bring cards in. The post box would be opened on the last day of term.

Jake had got very excited about that, and I thought he'd enjoy spending an hour or so writing them out. God knows, he needed cheering up. He was clearly missing our walks in the park with Dylan and Tyson, though he was far too considerate to say so. He'd obviously sensed that something was wrong and was being very careful not to ask too many questions, although I knew he was bursting to know what had happened.

I was so lucky to have him. Life without Jake would be an empty life indeed.

As I stepped out of the shop, my heart thudded on spotting Dylan across the road. Shocked at the unexpected sight, I wasn't quick enough to react. I should have ducked back into the shop, but I couldn't make myself move. He'd just locked the door of a dark blue van, with the words D Anderson, Electrician on the side, when he looked up and his eyes locked onto me.

At first he simply stared, and I wondered if he'd try avoiding me, but a moment later he was dodging between cars as he ran across the road.

'Ellie.'

'Hello, Dylan.' My voice sounded a bit wobbly, and I cleared my throat.

'How are you? How are Jake and Baxter?'

'Fine. You?'

'I'm — I'm okay. I'm feeling pretty stupid, but other than that...' He smiled.

'It's a shame you couldn't make it on Sunday,' I said, trying to keep my voice steady. 'Jake was looking forward to it. I guess you were busy.'

He ran his hand through his hair, a sure sign he was stressed. 'Yes. Yes, I'm sorry I had to call off, but it was something that couldn't be avoided. I've had a lot on lately. Things will get better.'

I nodded, unsure of what to say next. 'Well, I'd better get off. I have to collect Jake from school.'

'I'd offer you a lift, but I have an appointment. I'm already a few minutes late.'

'It doesn't matter. It's fine.'

'Is it?' He took my hands, his face suddenly serious. 'Ellie, I'm so sorry about all that Tyson stuff. I'm an idiot. I shouldn't have lied to you about her. You do know that I'd never deliberately hurt you? You believe that?'

'I—' The little voice urged me to reply that I did believe him. He wouldn't hurt me. But, despite its urgent whisperings I couldn't finish the sentence. He cupped my face in his hands and I tried my very best not to melt, but it was difficult. I mean, he was looking at me so intensely, and he was so exceptionally gorgeous, and his eyes were so kind and his lips… were suddenly on mine.

I didn't have time to think about it. At the simple pressure of his kiss, I responded with shameful eagerness — only to reel back in shock as he pulled away and dropped his hands like he'd been burned.

'I'm sorry. I shouldn't have done that, but…' He shook his head. 'God, Ellie, you don't make it easy for me.'

Well, it wasn't exactly a walk in the park for me. Ironically.

'I'm not Liam, Ellie. You have to know that.'

His voice sounded desperate, and I gulped. 'I know. Are you all right to meet up on Sunday? You can still bring Tyson if you like. Or Mitzi, or whatever she's called. I'm sure Baxter is missing her.' I gave him a warm smile, but it soon died as he returned it with a stricken look. 'What is it?'

'I won't be able to come to the park for a while. I have things to sort out, and I'm going to be busy. It's just for a little while, Ellie, honestly,' he protested.

I tutted and turned away.

'I have to go.' I needed to leave. Fast. I hadn't a clue what was going on, or what the hell it was that he wanted after all.

Before I could move he put his hands on my shoulders, turning me back to face him. 'I just—' He looked around, as if he was hoping to see the answer he was searching for, written on a shop window or something. 'Will you trust me, Ellie? Please?'

Well, that was the million-dollar question.

I thought about Liam, about all his lies, about everything Jake and I had been through. Then I looked into Dylan's eyes and, despite it all, I nodded.

He pulled me to him, and for one moment, I allowed myself to be held, feeling the warmth of him enfolding me. I would trust the little voice, for now, at least. I would believe that this man was telling me the truth.

I had no real choice. I was in far too deep.

Chapter 11
Wedding Day

J ake looked so handsome in his suit that he reduced me to tears. I adjusted his tie and pushed his fringe back a little then kissed him.

'You look lovely. So grown up. I'm so proud of you,' I said.

Jake looked embarrassed. 'I wish you were coming with me, Mum. I won't know anybody there, except Dad and Laura, and they'll be too busy kissing and stuff.'

'Your grandma will be there,' I reassured him, though he didn't look too impressed by that. 'And maybe Auntie Clare will go, and your cousin Lewis.'

My voice faltered. I really wasn't selling it to him at all. Jake didn't like his father's relatives any more than I did, and he wasn't looking forward to the wedding. In fact, the only thing that had persuaded him to go was the promise of a buffet afterwards, and the reassurance that he could help himself to as many sausage rolls and cupcakes as he wanted.

'Are your shoes all right? They're not pinching you?' I'd told him repeatedly to walk around the flat in them, get used to them, but he hadn't taken much notice. I took a box of plasters out of the kitchen drawer and took two of them out, slipping them in his jacket pocket. 'Just in case they start to rub. You don't want blisters, do you?'

I smoothed down his hair for the umpteenth time then glanced at my watch. 'Your dad will be here in a minute. Are you all ready? Do you need the toilet?'

'No. I'm all right. What are you going to do this afternoon?' Jake's face was anxious. 'Will you be okay?'

'I'll be fine,' I reassured him. 'I might start wallpapering the kitchen if I can be bothered. Or I might start that new book I've been meaning to read for ages. I'll have a nice, peaceful afternoon. Don't you worry about me. Promise?'

He nodded but I could see he wasn't convinced. I turned away quickly, walking to the window to hide the tears that had suddenly welled up in my eyes. Honestly, I was getting so weepy lately. I really needed to pull herself together, but Jake had been worrying about me since the carol concert.

I'd told him I'd met up with Dylan and that he was too busy to meet us for a while, and he'd said nothing, but I knew he was confused about it. So, not only was I upset about Dylan, but I was also upset about Jake's feelings. Then there was the small matter of my ex-husband marrying the woman he'd left me for, not to mention the fact that they were expecting a baby together. And then there was this flat, which still looked rather dreary, no matter how many Christmas decorations I'd hung, or how many fairy lights I'd draped around the tree. No wonder I was weepy really.

'Your dad's here!' I turned away from the window, forcing a smile, and held out my hand. 'Come on. Let's go downstairs. We don't want to make him late for his own wedding.'

Jake seemed to hesitate before he took hold of my hand and reluctantly allowed himself to be led downstairs to the front door.

All dressed up in a new suit, Liam stood beside the car, looking smarter than I'd seen him in a long time. He nodded at Jake then handed him a little bundle, containing a burgundy rose, pine cone, fern leaf and red berries, all tied together with rustic-looking string. 'Here you go. Buttonhole for you.'

'Nice colour scheme. Very Christmassy.' I pinned it to Jake's lapel. 'There you are. You look marvellous, doesn't he, Liam?'

'What? Oh, yeah, yeah. Really grown up. Smart lad, aren't you?'

'Are you all right?' I wondered why I was asking him the question. Liam was getting what he wanted after all. It should have been him enquiring how I was feeling, though that was an unlikely prospect.

'What? Oh, yeah. Fine.'

He didn't look all right. He looked glum actually. No doubt he'd be feeling nervous. Public occasions never had been his strong point. Whenever we'd gone to parties or family weddings, he'd always skulked in the corner, not wanting to make small talk or engage with people.

'Who's your best man?'

He seemed uncomfortable. 'Haven't exactly got a best man. Two witnesses — Laura's brother and his wife. They're all we need really for a registry office.'

'Oh, right. Okay. Well, good luck with it all.'

'Do you mean that, Ellie?' Liam asked. 'I know it must be really difficult for you. It's good of you to let Jakey come.'

I was quite surprised at his sudden change of attitude. Marriage must have been mellowing him before he'd even got the ring on his finger.

'Of course. I hope you and Laura will be very happy.'

'Thanks. I appreciate that.' He hesitated for a moment, as if he wanted to say something else, then seemed to think better of it. 'Come on, young man. Get in the car. We don't want to be late, do we? God help me, my life won't be worth living if I'm not there before she is.'

They got into the car and, as Liam drove slowly away, Jake pressed his nose against the rear window, waving to me until the car turned out of the road.

I sighed and turned away, heading back into the flat. I needed to keep my mind off the wedding. There was no way I wanted to sit and brood, which I probably would if only I'd let myself. It didn't take long for me to realise, though, that it wasn't Liam, or the wedding, that occupied my thoughts, but Dylan. I kept replaying our last meeting, his assurances that he wasn't Liam, his promises that things would get better.

That kiss. Oh, that kiss.

Why had he ended it so abruptly? I thought about the moment in the school corridor. I'd been so sure he was going to kiss me then. I felt a frisson of excitement just remembering the expression in his eyes, and the way he'd moved so close to me that I'd felt the brush of his skin against mine. I wished I knew what he was thinking, what was really going on. Was it his parents' bad marriage that had scared him off? Was that the problem? If so, could he overcome his fears and take a chance on me — on us?

I needed to do something to take my mind off it all. Maybe I'd make a start on wallpapering the kitchen after all.

As I stood in the poky little room, though, surveying the bare walls that had taken hours to strip clear of the woodchip left by the previous tenant, I realised I didn't have the energy or the heart to tackle the chore today. Instead, I flicked on the kettle and took a mug from the cupboard. A cup of tea, a biscuit, and a good Christmas novel. That would help me while away a couple of hours.

Twenty minutes later, I'd downed a large mug of tea, eaten four biscuits, and read the same page of the book several times without taking a word of it in.

It was no good. I had to get out of the flat. I would visit Maddie. That was the best thing. I'd take Baxter a treat and have a gossip with my cousin. Wayne would be at the football match. His team was playing away, and he'd arranged to travel down to London with his pals and spend the whole day there. Maddie would probably be glad to see me. Anything was better than staring at those four walls and brooding about Dylan, and the romance that might never happen.

***

There was no answer when I rang the front doorbell of Maddie's house a short while later. I peered through the window, wondering if maybe Maddie was in the kitchen listening to the radio. She had a habit of dancing and singing along to the latest tunes when she did her ironing. Although, of course, she could have been out — perhaps doing a bit of Christmas shopping in town. There were only a couple of weeks to go after all.

I peered through the living room window and found it empty. The television set was switched off — proof that Wayne wasn't there at least. Wondering what to do, I took out my mobile phone and rang Maddie. If she was in town and alone, maybe I could meet her there. I didn't have enough money to go Christmas shopping — I'd already bought and wrapped Jacob's precious Thunderbirds toys and a few other presents for him — but I could stretch to my bus fares and a coffee in The Beehive. As the mobile continued to ring a thought struck me, and I peered through the letterbox. I could just about hear the dulcet tones of Olly Murs, Maddie's major crush, whose latest song was set as her ring tone. So Maddie was in, but where was she?

A faint bark came to me. Was that Baxter? He sounded too distant to be in the house. The garden! They must be in the garden. That was why Maddie couldn't hear me knocking or ringing the bell.

I put my phone back in my bag and headed to the back gate. Maddie's house was terraced, and to reach the back garden I had to pass a few more houses, then nip down the wide passageway that separated Maddie's block from the next. As soon as I turned into the passageway behind the gardens my heart sank. I could hear raised voices and the occasional bark from Baxter, as two women had a vicious argument. I recognised Maddie's voice right away. What on earth was going on?

As I opened the back gate, I took one look at the scene and almost left again. Maddie was in the middle of a bitter argument with Mrs Lancaster, who lived next door. Both women were trying to make their point in very loud and forceful tones, while at the same time attempting to gather up bits of clothing that were strewn on the path, and yelling at Baxter, who was chasing round and round the lawn with what looked like a pair of rather large Y-fronts hanging from his mouth.

'Baxter! Stop it now!' I made a grab for his collar and managed to pull him to a halt.

He dropped the underpants and stood there panting, looking suspiciously like he was laughing.

'Ellie, thank God.' Maddie sounded almost breathless. 'Baxter's really outdone himself this time.'

She handed Mrs Lancaster a pile of clothes and began to gather up the items that were lying on the path.

Mrs Lancaster glared at me. 'You ought to be ashamed of yourself, leaving an untrained dog here while you swan off to a swanky new flat. If you didn't want to look after him you should never have got him.'

'What?' I stared in some bewilderment at Maddie, who had the grace to blush and hang her head. 'What exactly has been going on here?'

'I'll tell you what's been going on here,' said Mrs Lancaster. 'That dog of yours has eaten half of my Stan's Christmas presents. Of all the places to leave my parcels, the stupid delivery man had to leave them on my back doorstep. I'm going to sue that company. Your mutt jumped over the fence and helped himself. Just look at it! Carnage!'

'Mrs Lancaster came around here to tell me what had happened,' said Maddie, 'and Baxter followed her. He pulled everything out of her arms, as she was filling me in with all the gory details, so everything that hadn't already been chewed ended up getting trampled into the mud.'

Her mouth twitched and I bit my lip. It wasn't funny. I mustn't laugh. But the sight of Baxter standing guard over a huge pair of underpants was quite amusing. Almost as amusing as the hammock-like bra draped over the water feature. Almost.

To my horror, Mrs Lancaster followed my gaze and pursed her lips, her face suddenly red.

'Always get new underwear for me and Stan for Christmas. That and a new nightie and pyjamas. It's a tradition. It's ruined now. And he's torn my Stan's Liverpool shirt. How can I give that to him now? Do you know how much those things cost?'

'I'm terribly sorry, Mrs Lancaster,' I said. 'I'm sure it won't happen again. Perhaps things aren't as bad as you fear?'

'Yes they are,' said Maddie, folding her arms. 'In fact, they're probably worse.'

I glared at her. 'You're not helping, Maddie!'

'Well, you should have heard the insulting things she's just been saying about me and you. I tried to be polite, but honestly, she was just plain rude. I've only got so much patience, you know.'

'You see! This is what I've had to contend with,' said Mrs Lancaster. 'Is there any wonder the dog behaves the way it does with someone like her in charge? You should never have left it behind. It's disgraceful. I've a good mind to call the RSPCA.'

'I don't think the RSPCA deals with abused underwear, Mrs Lancaster,' said Maddie. 'Now,' she retrieved the bra and Y-fronts and handed them rather gingerly, and with a distinct curl of the lip, back to her neighbour, 'you have everything back and I'm quite certain that you'll make damn sure you assess the damage and give me a full bill.'

'And what about that fence?' demanded Mrs Lancaster.

'What about it? For your information, that fence belongs to me, not you, so if you want me to put up barbed wire or something, you can forget it.'

Mrs Lancaster glared at her. 'You need to make this fence higher. I want six-foot fencing along here before the week's out, or I'll report you to the police and the council, and —'

'Yes, yes, whatever.' Maddie practically propelled her neighbour down the path and out of the gate. 'Call Ghostbusters for all I care. Just go.'

'I can't believe you were so rude to her,' I said, as we drank tea in the kitchen ten minutes later. Baxter lay quietly by my feet, obviously relieved to see me.

Maddie nodded at him. 'That's the most settled he's been since you left. He's getting worse, he really is.'

'He shouldn't have attacked her parcels,' I admitted, 'but you could have been more diplomatic about it.'

'Diplomatic? To her?' Maddie banged her cup on the table in disgust. 'I intended to be, of course I did, but you didn't hear the things she said. Stuff about me being a woman of loose morals, practically living with Wayne, and about how I was turning this place into some sort of refuge, and she never knew who she was going to be living next door to next, and how I ought to make up my mind if I was running a hostel for the homeless, or some sort of animal sanctuary. I mean, who does she think she is? The stupid delivery company shouldn't have dumped her parcels in the garden. It's their fault really. Anyway, it's my house! I'll have whoever I like here.'

'Yet you told her Baxter was my dog?'

Maddie looked sheepish. 'I was just trying to disarm her, that's all. Said the first thing that came into my head. Honestly, what am I going to do with him? I hate to admit it but the old bat's right. We're going to have to get six-foot fencing up, and that's more money and effort. Wayne's going to be thrilled.'

'What's it got to do with him?'

'Well, he'll be the one putting the fencing up. Besides…' Maddie took another sip of tea and shrugged. 'He's moving in with me.'

'No! I thought you said you didn't want him to?'

'I know. But then he didn't come round for a week, and I missed him. I mean, I really did. It's funny how you get used to someone, and they come to mean so much to you without you even realising.'

I couldn't argue with that. Taking a sip of tea, I tried to push thoughts of Dylan away. 'So, what about Baxter? Is Wayne all right about him?'

Maddie didn't look at me. 'Wayne doesn't like him. Don't get me wrong, he'd never hurt him, but he did say he's on his last chance. I can't tell him about today's antics. I'm going to have to come up with some story about wanting a garden makeover and including new fencing as part of that. I hope to goodness that Mrs Lancaster doesn't come out as he's working and stick her oar in. God knows what the bill for the damage will be. Bet she tries to fleece me. Well, I'll be demanding receipts, that's for sure. This is all I need right before Christmas isn't it?'

She reached over to Baxter and gave him a gentle pat. 'Hear that? You've got to be good from now on. You're in last chance saloon, okay?'

Baxter snorted and Maddie shook her head. 'Like he'll take any notice of that.' She looked at me. 'What are you doing here today anyway? Where's Jakey? Oh!' She clapped her hand across her mouth in horror. 'It's today, isn't it? The wedding? I'm so sorry, Ellie. I completely forgot. I'm such an idiot. How are you feeling?'

'I'm absolutely fine. The wedding doesn't bother me at all. You should have seen Jake this morning in his suit. He looked adorable. Liam brought him a buttonhole too. He's quite the handsome little man.'

'Who? Jakey or Liam?'

I pulled a face. 'Definitely Jakey. I don't think of Liam as handsome anymore.'

'Too busy thinking about Dylan?' Maddie watched

me with a sympathetic expression on her face. 'Nothing to report there?'

'Nothing. I've not heard from him since that day in town. I guess I'll just have to be patient. He asked me to trust him, and I'm trying to.'

'Wow! Real progress! You must be looking through the eyes of love.' She broke into a chorus of The Partridge Family song, and I nudged her.

'Shut up! I'm not in love.'

Maddie switched to the 10CC song of that title, and I couldn't help laughing. Even so, as I watched my cousin close her eyes and sway dramatically as she sang, I thought maybe the words to that song were quite appropriate. I was protesting far too much.

Chapter 12
The Blonde

The supermarket was heaving. I barely had time to draw breath between customers, as queues stretched far back down the aisles. Trolleys were piled high with frozen turkeys and tins of Quality Street, and the alcohol shelves were practically decimated. I smiled politely at a customer who was complaining that we'd run out of sprouts and assured her, through gritted teeth, that we'd be all stocked up again soon, whilst fighting the urge to scream as Shakin' Stevens wished us, "Merry Christmas, Everyone". Again.

'Bet you're ready for a cup of tea,' whispered Martha, my supervisor, as she replaced the till receipt for me halfway through the afternoon. 'See to this next customer and I'll put a notice up saying you're closing. Go and get a cuppa while you can.'

'Thanks, Martha.'

Sitting in the canteen fifteen minutes later, I glanced at my watch. Just gone two. Another two hours and the store would be closing, and I could go home. I stood up and headed back onto the shop floor, wondering if Maddie would have given Jake one of her

Sunday roasts for lunch, or if I'd need to cook something substantial for him when he got home.

It was good of her to have him at such short notice. I wasn't supposed to have been working that day, and they were usually good about not calling me in on the Sundays Jake wasn't with Liam, but it had been an emergency and Kylie had sounded quite desperate.

I'd be so glad to get home. I thought about the good old days when Sundays were a day of rest. Fat chance of that any more.

My checkout was at the far end of the shop, and quite a walk. I dodged fully loaded trollies, whining children and grumpy husbands, and ducked down the homeware aisle. I liked to look down there, imagining the things I could buy for the flat when I got the money to do so. There were some lovely wintry things in stock now, and I was desperate to add some homely touches to the place.

The Christmas decorations had improved the look of the living room substantially but come January, it would be back to the dismal gloom again. Some new cushions would cheer things up, and perhaps a rug? Maybe a purple heather colour would look nice and cosy? I paused for a moment, eyeing the throws, and wondering how much they'd be reduced to in the January sales.

As I turned to continue my journey back to the checkout, I stopped dead in my tracks. Just ahead of me, examining the bedding of all things, stood Dylan.

142

And he wasn't alone. Beside him, a young blonde woman in tight white jeans, a fake fur jacket — at least, I hoped it was fake — and high heeled boots, leaned over a half-full shopping trolley, issuing instructions as to which package she wanted him to pick up.

'That pink one there! The one with the patchwork effect. No, that's the double. Pass me the king-size, silly.'

Dylan obliged and they stood, heads almost touching, scrutinising the duvet cover and pillowcases. There was a familiarity between them, an intimacy that was unmistakable. For one brief, glorious moment, it occurred to me that maybe she was Colleen, Dylan's sister-in-law, until I remembered that Coll had hurt her foot. It had sounded like a nasty injury, and I couldn't imagine she'd be shopping already, let alone in high heels.

But surely if Dylan had something to hide, he wouldn't have risked coming to Maister's, the very place where he knew I worked? Except, Dylan knew I rarely worked weekends, and then only on the Sundays that Jake was at Liam's. He wouldn't be expecting me to be there today. He would assume he was safe.

Any lingering hope I'd had that there was a reasonable explanation for his behaviour was crushed completely when I heard the woman say quite clearly, 'Well, I like it. I hate that beige thing we've got on our bed. The pink looks really pretty.'

Dylan laughed. 'You've nagged me for months to

change the colour scheme in that bedroom. Could you really see me sleeping in a pink bed? Oh well, your choice.'

I didn't wait to hear any more. Panic seized me as I imagined him turning round and seeing me. I couldn't bear to think about it. I really didn't trust myself to stay calm if I came face to face with him — let alone the woman who was quite obviously the reason he'd cancelled our meeting that Sunday, and was also, no doubt, the reason he was so evasive lately and had been avoiding me.

'I'm not Liam, Ellie,' he'd assured me.

Well, maybe not, but he was just as bad. The little voice had been lying to me all along. I flew back up the aisle and cut through electrical goods instead, praying they'd choose another checkout to go to.

I'd had enough lies and deceit to last me a lifetime. Whatever Dylan wanted from me it was over. I had no intention of getting involved with someone like him ever again.

Chapter 13
Baxter Goes Too Far

I peered out of the bus window, seeing little through the pouring rain. It had been a long day at the supermarket, and I had a headache coming on.

Being wedged against the side of the bus by a large gentleman with three bulging bags of Christmas shopping on his knee didn't help. I barely had a third of the seat to myself. The bus was packed, and the buzz of voices seemed to be growing louder.

Somewhere a mobile phone rang, and someone struck up a conversation with the person on the other end of the line, seeming not to care that everyone on the bus could hear every word they were saying. Why did people speak so loudly into their phones, I wondered? The woman was practically shouting. Didn't she mind that everyone was party to the information she passed on about her recent doctor's appointment and what the urine sample had revealed? People were very strange.

I tried to see where we were, but it was difficult to tell as the window was so streaked with dirt and rainwater. I couldn't see a thing through the front window because of people standing, due to the lack of seats. I tapped the large gentleman on the arm.

'Excuse me. Where are we?'

He shrugged. 'Not sure, love. Hang on. Edna!'

A tiny, bird like woman sitting a few seats down on the other side of the aisle, practically buried under a pile of Tesco bags, turned her head. 'What?'

'Where are we?'

'Newton Street. Why?'

The man turned back to me. 'Newton Street. Do you need to get off?'

I nodded. 'I'm next stop. Can I get by, please?'

The man huffed and puffed, trying to gather his three bags of shopping together. Hooking the handles over his sausage-like fingers, he struggled to his feet and tried to stand back, but people were blocking the aisle, and he knocked into someone who complained, quite loudly. He apologized and tried again to move back. I managed to squeeze through and stand in the aisle but getting through the numerous passengers who'd had to stand, clutching their Christmas shopping to them, proved more difficult than I'd anticipated. I caught a glimpse of my flat as the bus went sailing by and tried desperately to reach for the bell.

'The bell! Can you ring the bell please?'

A young woman, standing by a buggy, stared at me blankly. Her hand was cupped over the bell on the post. 'You what?'

'Can you ring the bell? I'm going to miss my stop. Oh, hell.' I made it to the front of the bus, just as it passed my stop. 'Can you pull over please? I was supposed to get off there!'

'Sorry, love. Can't stop now. Not 'til the next official stop. You should have rung the bell,' said the driver helpfully.

I gritted my teeth and clung on as the bus rattled on.

'Do you want this next stop?' enquired the driver eventually.

'You know I do.'

'Well, you haven't rung the bell,' he pointed out.

I took a deep breath and gave the young mother a pleading look. Reluctantly, she removed her hand, and I pressed the bell. The bus slowed and, thankfully, I managed to squeeze past a group of four or five passengers who were trying to get on. Honestly, how many people was he going to let on there, I wondered? They were already packed like sardines in a tin.

Stepping out onto the pavement, I hitched up my bag, grateful to be on solid ground again, even if it did mean I had to walk back up the road in the pouring rain. I'd almost finished papering the kitchen, and I was certain I could complete the job that evening before Jake got home.

It already looked so much better in there. I'd managed to save up enough for a new blind for the kitchen window, and a lightshade that matched. It would look much more cheerful when it was done. If I hurried I could get the blind fixed and the lightshade up that evening too. Then, I thought, it would be time to start on the bathroom — which, I knew, really would be a difficult job. Maybe I'd wait until after New Year.

'Ellie! Thank God. I thought you weren't coming back. I saw the bus go by, and you didn't get off, and I was worried—'

'Maddie?' She looked awful. She was soaking wet through, and her face was lined with worry. 'What on earth's wrong?'

'It's Baxter. He's done the most awful thing he could possibly do. I really don't know what to do with him.'

'You'd better come in and tell me what's happened.' I fumbled in my bag for my keys and began to unlock the front door.

'Hang on!' Maddie ran down the steps and splashed across the road to where her car was parked. I watched in surprise as she opened the door and let Baxter out onto the wet pavement.

'Why have you brought Baxter? You know I'm not allowed dogs in the flat.'

'Please, Ellie. It will only be for an hour or so. I couldn't leave him with Wayne. I dread to think what would have happened.'

Sighing, I moved aside to let them into the dark hallway. Baxter sniffed the air, not altogether approvingly. I couldn't really blame him. I'd never seen the downstairs tenants, but a horrible smell emanated from their flat, like soggy cabbage, dirty socks, and mould, all rolled into one. I'd never heard a vacuum cleaner or a washing machine coming from there. I dreaded to think what lay behind the door.

'Come on. Upstairs quickly,' I muttered, shutting the front door after me and hoping that Baxter wouldn't bark and alert anyone to his illegal presence.

The flat was even darker and drearier in the moody weather. The small windows didn't let much light in anyway, and on a day like today it was shrouded in gloom. I did what I always did as soon as I got home, to cheer the place up. I switched on the lamps in the living room, plugged in the Christmas tree lights, and turned on the fire and the television, lowering the volume. God help me in January when the fuel bills would arrive.

'Cup of tea?'

'Please.'

Maddie told Baxter to lie down and be a good dog then followed me through to the kitchen, looking around approvingly at the almost fully repapered walls. 'Wow! That looks much better. Makes quite a difference doesn't it?'

I filled the kettle and flicked the switch. 'I think so. It will look even better when I get the blind and the new light shade up. But never mind all that, what's going on with Baxter and Wayne?'

Maddie nibbled her nail pensively. 'Well, you know Wayne moved in officially on Saturday?'

I nodded.

'Yeah, well, he took this week off work so he could get settled in and do some odd jobs around the house. He's put the new fencing up, by the way,' she added. 'He couldn't see why we needed any, 'til I showed him the broken panels and the leaning post.'

'You didn't have any broken panels and a leaning post,' I said.

'Not at first, no. Took me absolutely ages to achieve that,' said Maddie. 'Honestly, the things I do to keep the peace for that dog. And look how he repays me!'

'How *does* he repay you? You still haven't told me what happened,' I pointed out.

'What? Oh, yes, well, Wayne was having a lie in, and I'd nipped to the shops. Thought I'd get some bacon and eggs and treat him to a full English breakfast. When I got back all hell had broken loose. Baxter had managed to nudge open the hallway door — my fault, I couldn't have shut it properly — and he'd gone upstairs and into our bedroom. Wayne was fast asleep and didn't hear a thing. He said he heard a kind of tearing noise in his sleep, and it must have woken him up. When he sat up, Baxter was lying at the side of the bed happily eating something. Wayne went to take it off him to see what it was, and—'

'What? What was it?'

Maddie raised her eyes to mine, and I clapped my

hand over my mouth. 'No! Tell me it wasn't—'

Maddie nodded. 'It was. Wayne's scrapbook. Absolutely ruined. He'd been looking through it before he went to sleep last night — not for the first flipping time, it must be said — and he'd put it on the floor next to the bed before he turned out the lamp. He's furious. Honestly, Ellie, when I got back I thought there'd be murder. He kept yelling that it would have been a collector's item one day, and we could have passed it on to our kids.'

I knew it was awful of Baxter, and it must be a very upsetting situation for poor Wayne, but I still had to turn away to hide a smile. Honestly, I was so wicked. No wonder things never worked out for me. Karma was always at work, no doubt about it.

'I know you think it's funny,' Maddie said.

I turned back to her, ready to apologise, but saw the twinkle in my cousin's eye and couldn't wipe the smile from my face. 'I'm sorry, I know it must be horrible for you, and I know it was a very wicked thing for Baxter to do, but—'

'But the thought of Wayne's scrapbook being a collector's item is just too amusing for you to pretend otherwise,' finished Maddie, nodding. 'I know. I had to stop myself from laughing at first. Wayne shouting about how he'd planned to put it on eBay one day was too funny for words, especially when not ten minutes previously he'd been insisting it would have been a family heirloom. Thing is, Ellie, it's not that funny anymore. Wayne's sick of him. He says if I don't do something with Baxter he'll be moving out again.'

'He doesn't mean it. Things will calm down.'

'I'm not so sure they will,' said Maddie. 'He's not a dog lover, and he's put up with a lot from Baxter lately. I don't suppose there's any chance that you could have him is there?'

'Are you serious?' I handed Maddie a mug of tea and shook my head. 'You know I can't possibly have him here. There's a strict no pets clause in the tenancy agreement. I think I'd be in trouble if the landlady knew he was here right now.'

'But he gets on with you and Jakey. He really misses you. His behaviour's just got worse and worse since you left.'

'You are still taking him for walks? I know I haven't been taking him out as much lately, and I'm sorry for that, but I still manage two or three days. What about you? You're taking him out the other days, right?'

Maddie looked guilty. 'It's not always that easy. I'm so busy, and he pulls so much. I can hardly control him. I can't always fit him in. But he's out in the garden a lot.'

'The garden's not big enough for him to have a really good run around and burn off that energy,' I said. 'No wonder he's being so naughty. He must be bored stiff.'

'Ellie, please think about having him,' pleaded Maddie. 'The landlady doesn't even live here. She need never know.'

'And suppose she found out? Suppose the tenants downstairs reported it? There's no way I could keep Baxter here without them hearing him. I can't risk being thrown out. Besides, look how small this place is. It would be impossible.'

'Well, can't you look for somewhere else? Somewhere bigger that allows pets?'

I gave her a withering look. 'It took me eight months to find this place, remember? Do you think I'd have moved here if I'd been able to afford somewhere bigger? I'm sorry, Maddie. Look, why don't you stay here for a couple of hours? Give Wayne time to calm down a bit. Then you can go home and try to soothe things over between him and Baxter. I'll start taking him for walks every day again, I promise. Tell Wayne that and tell him that it will burn off his excess energy and make him behave better. Just make him give him another chance.'

'Will you be able to take Baxter for a walk every day?' she asked doubtfully.

'I can't say whether it will be morning or evening, because it depends on my shifts, but I'll fit a walk in every day somehow.'

Maddie looked shamefaced. 'I'll try to take him out for extra walks too when I can. I should never have got him should I?'

I sighed. 'No, not really. You've never had a dog, and you had no idea how much of a commitment they are. You really didn't think it through. But you were only trying to do a kind thing. Don't feel too bad about it, Maddie. You've got a good heart.'

'Thanks. So, any news on the Dylan situation?'

I didn't know how to tell her what I'd learned. I felt such a fool for being taken in again. Hesitantly I confessed about the awful discovery I'd made on Sunday.

Maddie listened, her mouth dropping open in shock. 'Never! I can't believe it. And he sounded so nice. Just shows you. Are you positive she couldn't have been a relative? Or a friend maybe?'

'There was something — I don't know — intimate about them. You know that familiarity that couples get? I got the feeling they'd pushed a supermarket trolley around together many times before. Besides, they were discussing their bedding, their bedroom colour scheme.'

'What a rat-bag. I'm so sorry, Ellie. I feel partly responsible. I should never have tried to persuade you to give him a chance. You should have listened to your famous little voice.'

'That's just it,' I said gloomily. 'I did. Guess even my own little voice is lying to me now, and if I can't trust that what can I trust?'

Chapter 14
An Unexpected Visitor

Maddie peered out of the living room window. 'The rain's stopped. I think I'll get off now. Maybe Wayne's calmed down. Thanks for the drinks, Ellie.'

'Thanks for helping me finish the papering,' I said, smiling. 'And thank you, Baxter, for being so quiet and not getting up to any mischief while we worked.'

'I know. Unbelievable isn't it! You'd never think he could be so naughty at home. Well,' Maddie said, buttoning up her coat then clipping Baxter's lead to his collar, 'let's go and face Wayne. Hopefully, he'll have calmed down. He may have rung round his old football mates, as I suggested. They may have some stuff they can give him. Maybe I can do him some photocopies at least.'

We headed down the stairs, and I opened the front door. 'Thanks again, Ellie. I — oh!' Maddie pulled a face and grabbed my arm. 'Looks like you've got a visitor.'

She turned away, leading a curious Baxter past Liam as he ran up the steps to the flat. I heard him greet my cousin, but Maddie only acknowledged him with a faint nod of the head. Baxter tried to investigate further but she pulled him firmly away and across the road to her car. As she let him into the back seat, she peered across at me and mouthed the words, 'You okay?'

I nodded and waved, then turned to Liam. 'I'm afraid Jake's not in. He's gone for tea at Clare's.'

Liam's sister, Clare, had proved to be a godsend. To my astonishment, Jake and Lewis had really hit it off at the wedding, and Clare showed no signs of being anything like her brother, thank God. It was a shame that I hadn't got to know her better when I was married to Liam, but their mother had fallen out with Clare, and Liam always took his mother's side. It was a miracle that he'd overruled her and invited her to his wedding, one that had paid off for me, as well as Jake.

'I know. She mentioned. It's not Jake I've come to see. I need to speak to you, Ellie.'

I watched Maddie drive away then shifted aside to let Liam in. What could he possibly want to speak to me about? The only thing we had to discuss was his access visits with Jake, and he surely didn't want to cut those back even further? But then, if he did, he wouldn't bother to visit me to tell me. It would be a phone call or, more likely, a text.

I led him upstairs and gestured for him to be seated while I headed into the kitchen and flicked the kettle on yet again. Taking in the kitchen I smiled. At least it looked more homely and a bit lighter. One thing achieved at any rate.

Five minutes later I handed Liam a mug of tea and sat opposite him in the armchair. 'So, what can I do for you?'

Liam took a mouthful of tea, wincing like the hot liquid had scalded his throat. He put the mug on the coffee table and looked at me mournfully. 'Laura lost the baby.'

'Oh, Liam. I'm sorry to hear that.'

I was too. Nobody deserved to go through such pain. I knew how lucky I was to have had Jake. What would my life have been like without him? Poor Laura.

'Is Laura all right?'

'What? Oh, yeah, yeah. She's made of strong stuff you know. She's already talking about trying again.'

'Oh, right.' I supposed everyone handled things in different ways. I wondered exactly why Liam had come to see me. All right, losing their baby was sad, but he had friends and family. Why tell me specifically? What did he want me to say?

'Thing is, I don't want to try again.'

I took a sip of my drink. Surely, he hadn't come round to ask my advice about how to break it to Laura that he didn't want more children? It came as no surprise to me, given that he'd resisted all my pleas to add to our family. I would have been more surprised if he'd been enthusiastically planning more children. He peered across at me, a strange expression on his face. What was wrong with him?

I shifted uncomfortably. He was making me uneasy. I wished he'd just go.

'Well, you'll just have to tell her, won't you? You need to discuss it with her. It's none of my business, Liam.'

'But I can't discuss it with her, that's the thing.' Liam looked thoroughly miserable. 'She's not like you, Ellie. She doesn't listen. She just talks over me. Her and her mother. Christ, what a pair they are. I don't get a word in edgeways.'

I hid a smile. *Welcome to my world*, I thought. So, Laura was no pushover. Well, good for her. Despite everything that had happened I was glad she had the strength to stand her ground. She was so young — not much older than I'd had been when I married Liam. She could easily have submitted to his will the way I had. I couldn't help but admire her.

'It's nothing to do with me, Liam,' I told him. 'I don't understand why you're here. You should be talking to Laura.'

I stood, meaning to take my mug into the kitchen. I didn't feel like drinking more tea. I just wanted him to go and leave me alone.

He reached out and grabbed my wrist. 'I made a big mistake, Ellie. I know that now. When I look at you and Jakey, I see what I've lost. I don't know what happened, why I did what I did. There's only ever been you, Ellie, you know that. Laura was a massive error of judgement. I miss you. Give me another chance.

Please.'

Was he serious? The desperate expression in his eyes told me he very much was. I couldn't believe it.

'Your wife has just lost her baby, Liam. *Your baby.* Go home and take care of her.'

'She'll be fine. Her mother's there. Her mother's always there. Look at me, Ellie. I'm still the man you fell in love with. Can't you see that?'

I looked and could barely suppress a shudder. 'You're right, Liam. You are the man I fell in love with. You haven't changed a bit. That's why I know I wouldn't go back to you if you paid me a million pounds. You're still the same lying, cheating, selfish, weak man you always were. You've barely been married for five minutes. Your wife has just suffered a miscarriage, yet you're round here begging me to take you back after everything that you've done. Look at this place! This is what you've reduced your son to living in because you were too busy spending our deposit money to impress your girlfriend. You didn't care what happened to him, you didn't care what happened to me. Now there's not a sign of grief for the baby you've lost, or for the wife who's gone through such a bloody awful experience. Why the hell would I want you back?'

'You make it sound so black and white,' Liam whined. 'It wasn't like that…'

'I think it was exactly like that. Now can you go please? I have a blind to hang and a lightshade to put up before Jake gets home.'

'I could help you while we talk?'

'I don't want to talk, and I don't want your help. Just go.'

Liam's eyes narrowed. 'Is this about that Dylan bloke that Jake keeps banging on about? Are you seeing him?'

I flushed. 'No, I'm not seeing him. But if I was it would be absolutely none of your business would it? We're divorced, Liam. Now go home and take my advice. Try to sort things out with Laura and be honest, otherwise you'll have another divorce under your belt before the year's out, and two in one year is a bit much, even for someone like you.'

Liam's lip curled in disgust as he got to his feet. 'You're absolutely right. I don't know what I was thinking, coming round here. I guess the miscarriage has messed with my mind. It must have done to make me think I could ever be happy with you. I forgot, for a moment, how horrible it was living with you. Thank God you reminded me. I'm going home to my wife, and I'm going to take her the biggest bouquet of flowers that I can buy.'

'Good for you.' I shut the door behind him and heaved a sigh of relief. Thank God he'd gone. His final rant hadn't touched me at all. Nothing he said meant anything to me whatsoever.

I smiled and hugged myself as I realised I was truly free of him. He couldn't touch me any longer. I should have listened to my instincts from the start. I'd known what sort of man he was from our first meeting, but I'd ignored that little voice warning me, because I'd wanted to believe in him. Well, I'd never ignore it again.

As fast as it had arrived my smile faded, and I sank onto the armchair, full of confusion. That same little voice had trusted Dylan. From our very first conversation it had whispered to me that he was a man I could believe in. What was going on?

I'm not Liam, Ellie. His words replayed in my mind over and over, and I knew he was right. He wasn't Liam. So what had happened? What was he playing at? I shook my head, impatient with myself. Whatever there had been between us, it was over. As if to prove my point, I took out my mobile phone and, after a moment's hesitation, I deleted Dylan's number in a gesture of defiance. No going back.

Chapter 15
A Shock Discovery

The park was fairly empty, which wasn't surprising given that it was a cold, overcast Saturday in late December. The sky was heavy with snow, and I was pretty sure we'd have a layer of the white stuff covering the ground by morning.

Jake was very excited by the prospect of a white Christmas. Only a few days until Christmas Eve after all — something he reminded me of every five minutes. There were only a handful of doors left to open in his advent calendar, and he'd been to the class Christmas party at the end of term, taking with him my contribution — a large Yule log, which I'd shamefully bought at discount from work, having had no time to make anything myself — and he'd returned home with a stack of cards from his friends. He was looking forward to the big day.

I wished I could share his enthusiasm. My gloved hand folded around the piece of paper in my pocket, and I felt a lead weight pressing on my chest, suffocating me. Jake's Christmas list.

I'd been prepared for him to ask for things I

couldn't afford — although I'd managed to get his main presents and a few bits and pieces — but I hadn't expected the impossible to be on the list!

Dear father crismas
for crismas I would like a nice house, mum to be happy, a baby brother or sister because mine is in heven now, Baxter to live with us, Thunderbird 3, selecshun box or tin of rosies.
Thank you and merry crismas.
Love Jake Jackson xx
PS I hope you enjoy the mints pies and please give Rudolph the carot. xx

How was I supposed to make those wishes come true? Yes, a selection box and a Thunderbirds toy were among the presents already wrapped and hidden in my wardrobe, but how the hell did I make the first four things happen?

Jakey was going to be one disappointed little boy on Christmas morning. His life wasn't *Miracle on 34th Street*. There would be no happy ending for Jake. For either of us. I sat, trying hard to smile as he and Baxter had fun together — running races until Jake's legs were too tired to run any further.

Baxter, despite his panting, seemed capable of continuing indefinitely with his seemingly inexhaustible supply of energy, but instead he sat patiently while we fed the ducks then flopped at my feet as I sat on the nearest bench, watching my son play on the swings.

I wondered if Baxter was missing Tyson as much as I was missing Dylan. It wouldn't have mattered if the park had been heaving with people — I knew that it would always feel empty to me without him beside me.

Watching a couple, well wrapped-up against the icy wind, strolling hand-in-hand beside the lake, I tried to ignore the loneliness that suddenly attacked me. Was I destined to be alone for the rest of my life? Better that, I thought determinedly, than go back to Liam, or live with a liar for the rest of my life.

Try as I might, I couldn't think of a single plausible reason why Dylan would have been shopping for bedding with a glamorous blonde and discussing "our bedroom" if she wasn't his live-in girlfriend. Or wife. I sat up straight as that thought occurred to me for the first time. What if all that stuff about marriage and children had been a lie too? What if he was married and had made up all the stuff about divorce? What if he had kids? Oh, good grief. It was getting worse.

Seeming to sense my unease, Baxter whined, and I patted him and tried to calm myself down. Even if Dylan was a married man and a father I'd done nothing wrong. Well, there had been that kiss, and that almost kiss, but that was down to him. Besides, they'd been fleeting. So brief, they weren't worth thinking about. Moments that had been just that — moments. I should have been glad about that, not lying in my bed night after night, imagining how it would have felt if he hadn't pulled away so suddenly. If we hadn't been standing in a busy street but had been in my flat together alone, what would have happened next?

It did no good to think about it. I had to get on with my life and forget all about him.

Jake came over and sat beside me. 'Can I have a cookie, Mum?'

I rummaged in my bag, blinking away tears as I remembered all the Sundays when Dylan would produce some coins and hand them to my son, ruffling his hair and offering to get him a hot chocolate with plenty of whipped cream and marshmallows to go with his biscuit. 'Here. Get a plain one for Baxter, too,' I said, handing Jake some money. 'It might cheer him up.'

As he ran off towards the shop, I settled back in my seat and sighed. 'This is all because of you, you know that don't you?' I told Baxter. He stood up, plonked his heavy head on my lap and looked up at me with sad, brown eyes. 'If you hadn't come into our lives I wouldn't have brought Jake to the park that morning, and we'd never have bumped into Dylan. And we literally did bump into him, didn't we? Well, you did, anyway. Remember that, Baxter? Remember how you knocked poor Dylan flying? Do you miss him too?'

I fondled his silky ears, and he blinked. I thought it very likely that he did miss him. He'd absolutely adored him, there was no denying that. Seemed like all three of us had fallen under Dylan's spell. Jake returned and held out a biscuit to Baxter, who pounced on it eagerly.

'They're selling mince pies in there, Mum. Would you like one?'

'No, thanks, Jakey. I'm not hungry,' I said.

He sat down beside me on the bench, staring at his cookie but making no attempt to eat it.

'What's wrong?' I asked, desperate to see the smile return to his face. I nudged him. 'Hey, not long to go now, eh? Bet Father Christmas has got those elves working overtime, don't you?'

He sighed. 'Yeah.'

'What's wrong, Jake?' As if I couldn't guess.

He broke off a piece of cookie and examined it closely. 'It's not the same without Dylan and Tyson, is it, Mum?'

I swallowed. 'I — I suppose not.'

'Why did you fall out with him?'

'Who says I fell out with him?'

'You haven't seen him for ages. He never comes to the park with us anymore. I think Baxter's quite sad about that.'

'Is he? I expect he misses Tyson. I mean, Mitzi.'

'I think you're quite sad about it too.'

I stared into my son's bright blue eyes. He looked back at me, his face solemn. How did one so young understand so much? I squeezed his hand. 'It will be all right, Jakey. I promise. Things will get better.' I wondered who I was trying to convince — him or me.

***

'Can I get *The Beano*?' Jake asked as we passed the newsagent's on the way back to Maddie's house. I was dreading going back. The atmosphere in there had been awful when I'd collected Baxter that morning.

Evidently, things were still bad between Wayne and Maddie. My cousin had been forced to do an awful lot of grovelling, and she'd confided in me that Wayne refused point blank to even acknowledge Baxter, who'd been confined to the kitchen and garden whenever Wayne was in the house. I thought it was no wonder Baxter looked so depressed. What a way to live.

'Go on then. I'll wait outside. Be quick.'

I handed him some money, winding the lead around my wrist when Baxter tried to follow him. Mrs Wilson may have championed Baxter to Maddie all those weeks ago, but I doubted she'd welcome him into the shop. I peered at the goods on display in the window. Tinsel had been strewn across the glass, and Merry Xmas was written in spray snow. Everywhere I went it was the same story. Christmas was all anyone else seemed to think about.

Once I'd felt like that too. When I'd been living with Liam, and Jakey was a baby, we'd really pushed the boat out and I'd looked forward to Christmas so much.

But then I'd had a home. A family. It felt like Jake and I were just treading water, homeless, rootless. How could we enjoy Christmas feeling that way? Sighing, I patted Baxter as he pulled impatiently on his lead, then wandered slowly past the door to the second window.

There a notice board behind the glass, with several cards pinned to it. I glanced at them, only half paying attention. A second-hand washing machine for sale. A young girl offering babysitting services. Someone selling an ancient stereo system as an ideal Christmas present for the nostalgia fan. I stiffened, my stomach turning over, as I stared at the card in front of me.

Free to good home. Boxer dog, five years old. Good reason for parting.

The address was Maddie's. I couldn't take it in. What was Maddie thinking? She couldn't possibly give Baxter away. He'd already lost one home. He couldn't lose another.

As soon as Jake came out of the shop, clutching *The Beano*, I grabbed his hand.

'What's the matter?' he asked, clearly surprised.

'Come on, Jakey. We must hurry. I need to speak to Maddie — fast.'

***

Maddie looked over her shoulder and whispered, 'Wayne's in. It's not a good time to talk about this.'

'I don't care if it's a good time or not. What are you playing at? You can't just pass him on like some unwanted Christmas present. He's already been through this once before, remember?'

'Of course I remember. It was me that took him on wasn't it? And I did try my best, Ellie, you know I did. I just can't make him behave himself. You'll never believe what happened this morning.'

'Try me,' I said grimly.

She tutted. 'He only cocked his leg up against the Christmas tree and fused the bloody lights. Honestly. Right in front of Wayne. If I didn't know better I'd swear he did it on purpose to wind him up. Well, it worked. Wayne went mad. It's him or Baxter, and what can I do?'

'You do know you're doing the same thing his previous owner did? Choosing a partner over Baxter? The very thing you were so disgusted about!'

'I know, I know. You don't have to tell me. I feel bad enough as it is. Do you honestly think I don't feel guilty about all this? I tried, Ellie, but there's nothing I can do about it. If only Baxter was better-behaved, or a bit smaller. I can't force Wayne to like him, and if he's going to carry on eating scrapbooks, wrecking Wayne's jeans, stealing neighbours' belongings, and peeing on Christmas trees — well, it's his own fault. I'm sorry but that's the way it is.'

'I don't believe this.' I looked pleadingly at Maddie. 'Just think about it please. Don't give him away to just anyone. He needs a proper, caring home. Please don't rush into anything.'

'I won't.' Looking uncomfortable, she took Baxter's lead from my hand and ushered the dog inside. 'Thanks for taking him to the park. See you tomorrow?'

I couldn't speak. I was too sickened to reply. I turned and guided Jake down the path and out of the gate, not looking back at my cousin. I heard the front door shut and realised I'd been holding my breath. I let it out with a big sigh. Now what?

'What will happen to Baxter?' Jake's face was pinched with anxiety, his eyes wide with fear. 'What if somebody cruel gets him?'

'That won't happen. Maddie will check the new owner very carefully,' I assured him. Would she though? Or would she be so relieved to find a new home for him that she'd let him go to just anyone, the way his previous owner had?

'We've got to take him,' said Jake. 'Please, Mum. He can live in our flat. He'll be good, I promise. He loves us. He'll behave.'

'I'm sorry, Jakey. I can't do that. You know I can't. We're not allowed pets in the flat. If the landlady found out she'd make us leave, and then where would we go?'

'She won't find out. She never comes round.'

'But the other people who live in the house would hear him, and they might tell her.'

'He'd be quiet, I promise! He won't bark. He only barks if he gets upset or frightened, and he wouldn't be upset or frightened with us would he?'

'Jakey, he'd go insane cooped up in that tiny flat—'

'We'd take him for walks all the time!'

'Not all the time. How could we? I'm at work, you're at school. He'd be bored in there, and you know how destructive he gets when he's bored. Besides, we don't have the room for him.'

'He could sleep on my bed. I wouldn't mind. Please, Mum, please. Don't let them send him away to strangers.' Jake's eyes were bright with tears.

I gulped back tears of my own and squeezed his hand. 'I'm sorry, Jakey. I can't let him live with us. I wish I could, really I do. Maddie will find him a good home, I'm sure of it. Please don't worry.'

He wrenched his hand away from mine and marched in front of me, head down. I knew it would take a long time for him to get over this latest blow. If I'd had the power to put it right I would have, but it was out of my hands. There was no one to turn to. Baxter's future was in real jeopardy and there was nothing I could do about it.

Chapter 16
Baxter Takes Control

Jake wouldn't eat his breakfast and pushed away his cup of milk untouched. 'You have to eat.'

I tried to keep the anxiety out of my voice. He'd barely spoken a word to me for the last two days since my refusal to take Baxter on. He'd also hardly eaten a thing. I'd no idea what I could do to make him understand that having a dog in our flat just wasn't an option, and finding alternative accommodation was out of the question for a long time.

'I'm not hungry.' He stood up and grabbed his coat. 'Ready.'

He wasn't even excited to wake up that morning and discover a thick layer of snow on the ground. Usually he'd have been jumping up and down, demanding to go out and play in it.

With my heart breaking, I put his dish and cup on the draining board and picked up my bag and keys. 'Right. Come on then.'

We walked to Clare's house, not speaking. The only sound was the crunching of snow under our feet. He didn't even throw a snowball at me, which was unheard of. It was so unlike Jake to be quiet. Usually I couldn't halt his flow of chatter when we went out. Occasionally I'd longed for him to stop talking for a while. Right now, I wished with all my heart that he'd launch into one of his long discussions about something he'd read in *The Beano*, or which Thunderbirds character was the best, or what David had said in class last week that had made the teacher send him out to see the headmaster for the umpteenth time that term.

As we neared Clare's house, Jake suddenly turned to me. 'What if he's already gone?'

'I shouldn't think so. Maddie never mentioned anything when we dropped him off last night after his walk did she? I'm sure if she'd had a reply to the advertisement she would have told us.'

'She might not in case we stopped him going.'

I rubbed my forehead. 'We can't stop him going, Jake. I'm sorry, but I've already explained this to you.'

'Will you go and check? Make sure he's still there?'

'I have to go to work. You know I have to be there soon, and I'm working until six. That's why Auntie Clare's having you today.'

'After work? Before you come for me? Will you?'

I hesitated but nodded. It would mean a detour, a walk in the snow, and after eight hours at the supermarket I could have done without it, but if it would put Jake's mind at rest, even temporarily, it would be worth it.

'Thank you.' Jake's voice was small as he shuffled down the path towards Clare's front door, his head hanging low.

Clare opened the door, her face wreathed in smiles. 'Come in, Jake. Lewis has been waiting for you. Fancy building a snowman? I've dug out an old scarf and hat for him to wear.'

Jake nodded, pushing past her, and entering the house without looking back.

Clare raised an eyebrow and I shrugged. 'He's not having a good day. It's Baxter. I'll tell you later. Could you… Could you keep an eye on him? Try to cheer him up?'

'Of course. Don't worry. Lewis will have him laughing in no time.'

Somehow I doubted that. I said goodbye and turned away, wanting to cry for him. I only hoped I really could put his mind at rest and wouldn't have bad news to tell him that evening.

***

'You can't be serious.' I felt the colour drain from my face as Maddie broke the news to me.

'Tomorrow morning. They came to see him earlier and loved him. It's a good home, Ellie. He'll be happy there.'

'How do you know it's a good home? Have you inspected it?'

'Inspected it?' Maddie rolled her eyes. 'I'm not the RSPCA. Look, they were a nice couple, and they said they're keen on Boxers. They've read up on them and everything. I'm sure he'll be fine.'

'Read up on them? So, they've no experience with the breed? Have they got any experience with dogs at all? Have they owned a dog before? Do they understand the level of commitment needed?'

'Of course they do. They've read some books about it. They're taking it very seriously. They haven't had a dog before, no, but everyone's got to start somewhere. Everyone has to have a first dog, don't they?'

'But I don't think Baxter is the ideal first dog, do you?' I desperately searched my cousin's face for some sign that she was having doubts. 'It's Christmas, Maddie. You know what they say. A dog is for life, not just for Christmas. They've probably got carried away, thinking he'll be a nice present for them, but the novelty will wear off. Please, you must see what a bad idea this is. At least wait a couple of months—'

'Look, Ellie, he's going tomorrow morning, and that's that. I'm sorry but there's nothing I can do about it. Wayne's already agreed with them, and—'

'Wayne! I might have known. Did you actually see them? Did you talk to them?'

'Of course I did! Honestly, I'm not like Baxter's previous owner, you know.'

'Aren't you? I'd think about that one, Maddie.'

Maddie tutted. 'Okay, if you're going to be like that

175

you may as well go.'

She began to shut the front door, but I stuck my foot in the gap and prevented it from closing. 'Wait! Can I take him for one last walk? Please, Maddie. Just to say goodbye?'

Maddie opened the door again and folded her arms. 'Promise you're not going to do anything stupid?'

'Like what? There's nothing I can do! Don't you think if I had a choice, I'd have taken him by now?'

'Hmm. I suppose so. Okay then. Wait there. Wayne's having his tea and it's probably best you don't come in now.'

I was quite relieved to hear it. I didn't trust myself to face Wayne, not feeling the way I did. If I'd had my way it would be his chestnuts roasting on an open fire over Christmas, and I was far too tempted to tell him so. Unfortunately, mine and Maddie's relationship might never recover if I did.

'There you go.' Maddie handed me the lead, and Baxter leapt out of the front door onto the path, almost as if he couldn't wait to escape. 'See you later.'

She closed the door, and I followed Baxter, who pulled hard on the lead, out of the gate. Evidently he wasn't worried about a couple of inches of snow.

I couldn't believe it was the last time I would ever take him for a walk. How could Maddie bear to let him go? All right, he had his naughty moments, but that was more from boredom than anything. He was a sweet, loving dog, who just needed to feel loved and wanted. How could Wayne and Maddie not see that?

Tears pricked my eyes as I walked, wondering about the couple who were going to collect him the following morning. Would they be good to him? Would they understand him? Or would his excess energy, his low boredom threshold, and his general bounciness infuriate them before long, as it had Maddie, and lead to him being passed on to yet another home? What would become of him?

Jake would never forgive me for Baxter's rehoming, I thought anxiously. If only Dylan was there, he would know what to do. I'd thought, many times over the last couple of days, that if only I'd got his address, or kept his phone number, I could have contacted him about the situation. Even if the two of us weren't together and never would be, it didn't alter the fact that Dylan was very fond of Baxter, and Baxter obviously adored him. Dylan owned his own house and didn't have a dog already. He might have been persuaded to take Baxter on. Why had I been so stubborn and so stupid that day and deleted his number, just to prove a point? I was an idiot. Now I'd robbed Baxter of the one chance he might ever have had of a good home. Really, how could things get any worse?

Baxter stopped dead suddenly and sniffed the air. I blinked and looked round. Where were we? Good grief, he'd led me to Glamis Avenue again. Oh God, he'd caught the scent of that cat hadn't he?

I made a lunge for his collar but was too late. Baxter

leapt forward with such speed that the lead was yanked from my grasp, and I yelled at him as he bounded away from me, the lead trailing uselessly beside him. I began to run, slipping and sliding in the snow, cursing my heeled boots and the weight of my bag as I watched him streak along the pavement towards the pretty bungalow at the end of the block, where the cat that had tormented him so cruelly lived.

I gulped when I saw him stand still, facing the gate. My stomach churned as he gave a delighted bark then my legs almost gave way in fear when he took a flying leap over the hedge into the garden.

'Oh God, no! No!' Fearing carnage, I ran as fast as I dared, my lungs straining as I charged towards the bungalow.

'Baxter, get here. Get here now!'

I reached the bungalow and stood still, my hand clutching my side where I'd developed a stitch. My breath came in gasps as I took in the scene in front of me. The pink mobile nail van had gone, and in its place was a dark blue van with the words D Anderson, Electrician in white script on the sides. There was no sign of any cat, but Baxter probably wouldn't have noticed if there had been. He was too busy bouncing up and down like Skippy the bush kangaroo, smothering a delighted Dylan with kisses.

'I — I don't understand.'

Dylan? Was he doing some work at the bungalow then?

He looked up and saw me standing there, totally confused.

'Ellie. It's so good to see you. Both of you.'

'Are you — are you working here?' I looked round, baffled.

Dylan gave me a gentle smile, and despite everything my stomach fluttered. 'No. This is where I live.'

'You live here?' I gulped and peered through the window, expecting to see the blonde woman appear at any moment. So it was Dylan's girlfriend who had the pink van. Dylan's girlfriend who had the arrogant cat. Well, just when I'd thought things couldn't get worse, they had to go and prove me wrong. Now I not only had the image of his girlfriend in my mind, but I could picture them together in their bungalow. Their pretty, whitewashed bungalow. Their sweet bungalow that I'd loved the moment I set eyes on it.

God, life was harsh sometimes.

And to top it all off, there was no way Dylan could take Baxter after all. Not with that cat in the picture.

Dylan managed to prise Baxter off him and crunched down the path, opening the gate for me. 'Come in. Please. I'll make you a coffee.'

My insides turned to liquid. 'What about — I mean, are you alone?'

He looked surprised. 'Yes. Completely. Will you come in? Please? You and I have a lot to talk about.'

Chapter 17
The Little Voice

I was trembling as I followed Dylan and Baxter into the bungalow, Baxter's tail wagging so hard I thought he'd take off at any moment.

I was torn between wanting to be with Dylan and the certain knowledge that I didn't want to see where he lived with his girlfriend, let alone come face to face with her. Sure, she may have been out right then, but what if she came back? How would Dylan explain me away?

Maybe he'd just tell the truth. That I was someone he'd met in the park, and we'd sometimes walked the dogs together. That was all there was after all. Well, apart from the kiss, and the nearly-kiss. Although, why had he borrowed his sister-in-law's dog in the first place? That could be tricky to explain away.

I wondered if he already had a cover story planned.

He led me into a large, comfortable lounge and motioned for me to sit down. Even though I was worried I couldn't help but notice how lovely it looked. A wood burning stove glowed from within a big open fireplace, and a holly garland, complete with red berries, had been draped across the mantelpiece. A real Christmas tree stood in a recess, filling the room with the fragrance of pine. It looked like something from a Christmas card, and I thought about my dingy flat again and cringed inside, glad that he'd never seen it.

I perched on the sofa, yelping when Baxter leapt up beside me.

'Baxter! Get down! I'm so sorry, Dylan, I don't know why he's done that. He never did it at Maddie's.'

'It's fine, don't worry. I'll get you that coffee.'

He headed into what was presumably the kitchen, and I sat, wondering what had happened, and how I'd come to be in such a position. Of all the coincidences! Baxter seeking out the cat that day, and all the time it had been Dylan's home. It was unbelievable really. And for him to lead me to the same house again today — amazing.

I frowned. Yes, it was amazing. And unbelievable. Something didn't make sense.

Dylan returned and handed me the coffee. I was surprised to see his hands trembling. So, he was nervous, too? Maybe he was worried his girlfriend, or wife, or whoever she was would come back early. I guessed I'd better drink my coffee and get out of there. Save us both an embarrassing scene.

'It's so good to see you, Ellie. I can't tell you how glad I am to have you here, to be able to talk to you properly. I've been trying to pluck up the courage to call you all week, but I was so afraid you wouldn't want to know. It's fate.'

I peered at him over the coffee cup. 'Is it? I'm not so sure about that.'

'You're still angry with me. I can't blame you after all that stuff with Mitzi, and then cancelling our meeting and not getting in touch for so long. Will you give me the chance to explain? To put things right?'

'I don't think so, Dylan. I don't think I want to hear any more of your lies.'

'My lies? You mean about Mitzi? Just one little white lie—'

'One little white lie?' I put the cup on the coffee table and glared at him. 'You really think I don't know?'

He frowned. 'Know what?'

'About a certain blonde woman who drives a pink van? A woman who does nails for a living. A woman who owns a very fluffy and rather spoilt cat called Cupcake. Bloody Cupcake, for God's sake! A lady who doesn't like the beige bedding you have in your room but is rather keen on pink patchwork.'

He looked stunned. For a moment he simply gaped at me then he ran his fingers through his hair and leaned back in the armchair, seemingly lost for words.

I felt a moment's satisfaction and took another sip of my coffee. 'I'm good, aren't I? Who needs Mystic Meg with me around?'

Dylan shook his head. 'I don't understand. How could you possibly know all that?'

I put down my cup and wrapped my arms around myself, trying to suppress the misery that suddenly engulfed me. He wasn't denying it. I should at least have been grateful for that, even though I had to acknowledge that a big part of me had been hoping he would. Evidently, I'd hit the nail on the head.

Trying to keep my voice steady, I explained about Baxter's last visit to Glamis Avenue, his desperation to get at the cat who was so clearly tormenting him, and about the voice of the woman I'd heard calling for her Cupcake. I then told him, not looking at him, about my unexpected shift at the supermarket, and how I'd heard him and the blonde discussing their bedding while I was standing only a few feet behind them.

Dylan stared at me in horror. 'My God, what you must have gone through! Oh, Ellie. I'm so, so sorry.'

'Don't be. It's just the way it is, and it doesn't matter.' I stood up and looked at Baxter. 'Come on, you. Time for home. Not that it will be home for you much longer.'

'Ellie, sit down. We have to talk about—' He stopped suddenly like my words had just sank in. 'What do you mean, it won't be home for him much longer?'

I shrugged. 'Maddie's decided she can't cope with him. She's giving him away to a couple who've never owned a Boxer dog before. Or any dog, come to that. God knows what will happen to him.'

And then the tears came. To my horror, I crumpled right in front of him and dropped back down on the sofa, holding my head in my hands as I sobbed.

'Ellie, don't! Don't.'

Next to me in a flash, he slipped his arms around me, stroking my hair as I valiantly tried to pull myself together.

'I'm all right. Please don't touch me.'

I didn't think I could bear it much longer. I'd wanted to feel his arms around me for so long, but now it was happening at last I just wanted him to go away. If he continued to hold me I would give in, I knew it. The blonde would cease to matter. I'd be lost.

'Do you really mean that?' His grey-green eyes were questioning, full of anxiety, and I knew it was already too late.

'No.' It was only a whisper, but it was enough. Suddenly he was kissing me, and I was kissing him back, and the little voice that should have been telling me to walk away while I still could was strangely silent.

'We can't do this,' I murmured, but he kissed me again, and I allowed myself to be pulled against him, a tremor passing through me as he cupped the back of my head and I melted into him.

Baxter leapt off the sofa and I emerged from my trance. 'Oh, God. Stop it, what are you doing?'

I pulled away from him, trying to steady my breathing as he stroked my face softly. Dimly, I was aware that Baxter had trotted out of the living room and was heading into the kitchen. I really should have stopped him, but Dylan's eyes seemed to have locked me in their gaze.

'Kissing you,' Dylan said in answer. 'Please don't stop me. I've been waiting to kiss you properly forever.'

'But what about your girlfriend? It's not right. You can't do this to her. You said you weren't Liam.'

I had to be strong. His morals were evidently non-existent.

'I'm not Liam. I'm nothing like him. You must know that. You do know that don't you?'

He pulled me towards him again and I yielded for a moment. There was no warning from the little voice. Evidently, it was so disgusted with me it had packed up and moved out. I was lost for a moment in a world where Dylan and I were together forever, and there was no blonde, no cat, no pink nail van, no beige bedding...

Something landed on my knee, and I stared down at the rather tatty, dribble-covered Father Christmas toy that Baxter had just dropped in my lap. 'What the—'

I leapt to my feet in horror. 'You have kids?'

'What? No, no, of course not! That's a dog toy.'

'Of course it is. Why would you have a dog toy when you own a cat?'

'I don't own a cat. Melissa owns a cat.'

'So, why would you have a dog toy?' Nothing made sense. If he did have kids I was leaving right now. More than that, I was leaving town. I never wanted to see him again. I didn't care what the little voice had said. Or not said.

'Because I used to have a dog, and this was all I had left of him. Oh, Ellie.' He ran his hands through his hair again and looked up at me, a desperate expression on his face. 'Haven't you worked it out yet? Baxter was *my* dog. *I'm* the irresponsible owner.'

Of course he was. That's what had been nagging away at me ever since I'd seen him in the garden. Why would Baxter have brought me to the same place twice? How could it be a coincidence that Dylan lived there? No wonder Baxter had been so delighted to see him that day at the park that he'd charged into him, knocking him over. No wonder he was so thrilled to meet up with him every day. No wonder Dylan had said all that stuff about Baxter letting Tyson win a race. He hadn't been talking about dogs in general. He'd been talking about Baxter specifically. They already knew each other.

Melissa! He'd just called his girlfriend Melissa. The blonde was the princess who wanted rid of Baxter.

'So not only are you an unfaithful boyfriend, or husband, or whatever, but you're also an uncaring dog owner too. Are there any more lies you'd like to confess to?'

'Okay, let's just get one thing straight. Yes, I was irresponsible and stupid letting Baxter go to just anyone, but I'm not uncaring. Far from it. And I'm not an unfaithful boyfriend. Nor am I an unfaithful husband. I'm not married. I've never been married. I told you that.'

'Then who is Melissa? And why didn't you tell me Baxter was your dog the very first time I saw you?'

He patted the sofa next to him and sighed. 'Sit down, Ellie. I promise I'll tell you everything.'

'Everything?'

'Everything.'

'From the beginning?'

He smiled. 'Promise.'

'Go on then.'

'Well, I suppose it all began with the fire. I'd been going out with Melissa for a couple of years. It was nothing serious. Neither of us wanted to settle down but we were having fun and it suited us both. Then there was a fire at her place. She wasn't hurt, thank God, but she lost most of her stuff and she wasn't insured.

'She needed somewhere to stay. So many people had been getting at us, nagging that it was time we settled down. We're both in our early thirties, after all, and apparently there's a law that says we should be grown up and make some sort of a commitment.

'Melissa and I had already agreed that neither of us wanted children. I didn't trust myself to be a good father, and she's not the maternal type. She said her cat was the only baby she needed. That suited me, so I finally asked her if she wanted to move in with me.

'She had nowhere else to go, and I suppose, like me, she was fed up with people nagging at her to settle down, so she agreed. Her mother said she'd look after the cat, as there was no way she could stay here with Baxter around. But Melissa had only been here a few weeks when she started to get this rash. It was all over her hands and she was adamant that she'd only got it when she'd been stroking Baxter. I didn't believe her at first. I told her to go the doctor's. She did, and when she came back, she said he'd confirmed that it was an allergy to dogs.'

'But one visit wouldn't have confirmed that,' I said scornfully. 'She'd have needed tests to see what the problem was. Anyway, surely she'd met Baxter before if you'd been together for two years?'

'She had, but she told me the doctor had explained that allergies can develop any time. She said we'd have to get rid of Baxter.'

'And you agreed? Just like that?'

'Of course not! I refused point blank. But her hands were so painful and raw, and she was getting in a real state about it. It wasn't going away, even though she was avoiding Baxter and washing her hands all the time in case she touched anywhere he'd been. It got to the point where she wouldn't let him in the lounge because she said his dog hairs on the carpet and sofa were causing a reaction. He'd always had free run of the bungalow. Suddenly, all the doors were locked to him. He was pretty miserable.'

I could imagine he had been. And sadly he'd gone through a similar experience at Maddie's, thanks to Wayne. It occurred to me, suddenly, that the allergies explained Melissa's Princess Grace look. No wonder she'd been wearing long gloves when Maddie collected Baxter.

'Anyway,' Dylan stood and wandered over to the window, staring out across the front garden, 'she said she knew a couple who were looking to give a dog a home. She said they'd had plenty of experience, that their dog had died a year previously, but they were now ready to take on another one. I wasn't sure. She brought them round one evening and they seemed genuine enough and really took to Baxter. I thought, maybe it would be okay, and I agreed to let them have him on a trial basis. If I couldn't bear it, or it didn't work out with them, Baxter would be returned to me.'

He turned to face me, and I saw the stricken expression in his eyes.

'Melissa was delighted that I'd agreed and kept promising me he would be fine, and I could still visit him whenever I wanted. He was supposed to be leaving at the weekend and I was dreading it. I spent all week psyching myself up for the big goodbye. Except, I never got to say goodbye. I got home from work one evening and he'd gone. Melissa said that the new owners had just turned up, asking if they could take him that day as they were going on holiday and wanted to take him with them so they could all get to know each other better. I was so shocked and upset I never thought how ridiculous that sounded. I just...'

'You just what?' I said gently, my sympathy for him spilling over despite everything.

He bit his lip and shrugged. 'I went to my room and shed a few tears. I admit it. It was all so bleak without him. I just wanted them to come home so I could see him. I started looking for him in all the old places I used to take him. Melissa was a lot happier, but it didn't take long for us to realise that her hands were no better. In fact, if anything, they were getting worse. Eventually she discovered she was allergic to some of the stuff she uses at work. Baxter had nothing to do with it. I said that meant we could get Baxter back, but she said she'd tried to contact the owners and they'd moved.'

He walked back over to the sofa and sank down beside me, shaking his head. 'I didn't believe her, and we started arguing. A lot. To be honest, it wasn't working out living together, and I think we both knew it. But she had nowhere else to go, and neither of us seemed to have the nerve to put it into words.

'She'd been nagging at me for ages to take up running, get fit. I'd always resisted because I couldn't think of anything worse, frankly. Then it occurred to me that it would be a great excuse to go to the park. It can look a bit dodgy these days can't it? A single man in a park full of children, I mean. But no one thinks twice about joggers, and it would be a great way to search for Baxter. If the new owners were still in the town they would surely go to the park regularly. I'm not good at running. I've never jogged in my life to be honest. It nearly killed me that day, just running out of the park after we said goodbye. I'm not as fit as I should be, clearly.'

I couldn't help thinking he looked pretty fit to me.

'Fortunately, I'd only been twice when I struck lucky. I found Baxter — or rather, Baxter found me. I was so thrilled to see him, but really puzzled that he was with you. You weren't one of the people who came to see him here. I was going to ask you what was going on, tell you who I was, but then you started ranting about the irresponsible owner who'd abandoned him to his fate, and telling me all about the card in the shop window and how nobody had even checked where he was going.'

I sighed. 'I guess I did go on about it a bit. It was because I was worried you'd sue me. I suppose I was making excuses for him and went a bit over the top.'

'Maybe you did, just a little.'

As I raised an eyebrow he threw up his hands. 'Not that I blame you. You had every right to rant. Anyway, by that point I was far too embarrassed to admit who I was, but you asked me if I wanted to meet up with you again, walk our dogs together, and it was a chance to see Baxter regularly, find out how he was, and make sure he was being looked after. I figured, after a little while, I'd come clean, once I'd persuaded you that I was a decent sort of person after all. Huh, really did well at that didn't I?'

He gave an embarrassed laugh, but I couldn't bring myself to respond. I'd thought he wanted to walk with us because he'd been attracted to me, when all the time it had been Baxter he'd wanted to see, not me. I felt so stupid.

'Anyway…' Dylan looked at me anxiously, but apparently felt it best to continue with his story. 'I came home, confronted Melissa, and discovered the truth.'

'Which was?'

'The couple who were supposed to be taking Baxter had backed out. The husband had been offered a job, but it came complete with living quarters and no dogs were allowed. They'd explained it all to Melissa, but she hadn't bothered to tell me. Her excuse was that she was beside herself worrying about her allergy and just wanted to act while I'd agreed to Baxter leaving, so she'd placed the ad in a few shop windows. She thought if I knew the couple had changed their minds, I'd change my mind too. She was quite right. I would have.

'It was all too late by then of course. And it was the final straw for me and Melissa. She'd moved that damn cat in, and between them they were driving me insane. I didn't know how much more of them I could stand, but I was trying so hard to be responsible and grown up, the way everyone wanted me to be. But then there was you, Ellie.'

He took hold of my hand. 'You were so easy to talk to, so good to be around. I found I was looking forward to visiting the park as much to see you as Baxter. And quickly, I realised I'd still want to see you, even if Baxter wasn't there. That said a lot to me, and it scared me.'

'Why did it scare you?'

'I've never wanted to get that close to anyone before. I've seen what a vicious divorce can do. I thought marriage inevitably ended in anger and pain and bitterness. I didn't want to go anywhere near it. Then I met you, and I saw the way you coped with everything Liam had done to you, and the way you kept things so civilised for Jake's sake, and I began to wonder if maybe things could be different. I loved being around Jakey. I could see myself having children of my own for the first time in my life.

'That night at the carol concert, being with you and him and Lucy... I let myself fantasise, for just a moment, that you were my little family. It felt so good. I didn't know what had happened. I only knew I wanted to be with you. You took the fear away. And that's when I knew I had to back off, fast.'

'But why? If you thought that, if you wanted me... You almost kissed me that night, and then you just pretended nothing had happened. And that day in town, you did kiss me, but you couldn't pull away fast enough. It was like it was all some dreadful mistake that you regretted. Do you know how much that hurt me?'

'How could I do anything else? You've been through so much with Liam and Laura. There was no way I was going to behave in the same way. I had Melissa to think of too. We weren't madly in love, but she was still living with me, and she deserved the truth. So I sat her down and explained it all to her.'

'Hmm. How much did you explain exactly?'

'Everything. The day after the carol concert, I told her I'd met someone who I thought I had a real future with. That's why I couldn't meet you that morning. I knew I had to be honest with Melissa. I told her that nothing had happened between us yet, but that I really wanted it to. I told her that, although I could hardly believe it myself, I could see the time coming when I wanted everything I'd run away from for so long. Marriage, even children. And I told her that it was all because of you, and how I felt about you.'

'But you never mentioned her to me all the time we were meeting up at the park,' I pointed out, folding my arms defensively.

'You told me Maddie had been here, that she'd met Melissa. I was worried that if I told you I was living with someone, things would get complicated — that I'd trip up somehow, mention her name or something, and you'd realise I was Baxter's owner. It was safer to not mention her at all. It wasn't that I was trying to deceive you because I was planning some sort of affair or anything. I wasn't. At first, I admit it was all about Baxter. Then I just wanted to spend time with you. As

194

a friend, I mean. I wasn't expecting to develop these feelings for you, or I'd have been honest from the start. With you and Melissa.'

I hesitated but the little voice stayed silent. I unfolded my arms and squeezed his hand. 'So, how did she take it?'

'She was okay about it actually. She was more worried about where she would live, but I told her there was no rush, and I'd help her find somewhere. And I did. We found a nice flat for her and Cupcake, and I lent her the deposit money. I even took her shopping to replace the stuff she'd lost in the fire.'

'Like bedding?'

He gave me a sympathetic smile. 'Like bedding. I'm so sorry you had to go through that. If I'd known you'd seen us I would have explained everything straight away.'

'Why didn't you tell me? After the carol concert at least.'

'I just wanted — needed — to get things sorted out properly before I told you how I felt. I didn't want you caught up in any mess. I knew you were suspicious of men after what Liam did, and I wanted everything to be up front from the start. I was afraid you wouldn't want to get involved with someone who had such a lot to sort out. I needed to wait until Melissa moved out before I told you how I felt. I was trying to be fair to you, so we'd have a clean page to start afresh, and I also wanted to be fair to her. I didn't think it was right to start a proper relationship when she was still living here. Do you see that?'

I could barely speak for the tears threatening to choke me. I reached into my coat pocket for a tissue, and a piece of paper fluttered onto my lap.

'What's that?' Dylan asked, obviously noting the childish writing.

I gulped. 'Jake's Christmas list,' I murmured. 'You can read it if you like.'

He picked it up and smoothed it out, and I watched the expression on his face change as he read what it was my little boy wanted most for Christmas.

'Bloody hell, Ellie.' He looked up at me and seeing the tears spilling over my lashes he took me in his arms again and held me tightly. 'It's been agony, waiting for Melissa to move out. I was so afraid you'd move on and forget me.'

'Forget you?' I laughed through my tears. 'I could never forget you. I can't think of anything *but* you.'

He cradled my face, his eyes shining. 'I love you, Ellie — you and Jakey. I would never want to hurt either of you, and I'll do everything I can to make you both happy if you'll let me. Will you let me?'

I gulped and nodded, and he wiped my tears and kissed my lips, and the little voice in my head finally spoke up and whispered *I told you so.*

Chapter 18
Miracle on Glamis Avenue

'Merry Christmas, Jakey.' Maddie wrapped her arms around him and smothered him in kisses. 'Has Santa been?'

Jake shrugged. 'He brought me a lot of stuff. I got a Thunderbird Three.'

'Well, that's great news.' Maddie stepped back and looked at me, raising an eyebrow in query.

I nodded. My little boy had been subdued all morning, and even his presents hadn't cheered him up. I had a feeling, though, that his day was about to get much better.

'Well,' she said brightly, 'I've got you some more presents in the car. Ooh, and I've got a special treat for you. Wait there.'

She hurried out of the room and Jake looked at me dully. 'She'd better not have brought Wayne with her.'

'Of course she hasn't. Wayne's at home, cooking the Christmas dinner. She's got him trained already,' I said laughing, but my laughter died at his solemn little face. I couldn't wait to see that expression change.

I glanced at my watch and felt my stomach flutter with joy. Not long to go.

'Here we are!' Maddie's voice floated through the wall and the door flew open again. Jake leapt up and shrieked with delight as Baxter hurled himself at him, frantically licking Jake's face and nudging him with his nose.

'Baxter! What are you doing here?' Jake beamed up at us. 'Has he come to live with us? Is he my present, Maddie?'

Maddie and I exchanged glances. 'Well, er... Hey, I can't smell any cooking in this flat,' said Maddie suddenly. 'Aren't you cooking a turkey?'

Jake tugged at my hand. 'Mum, we haven't got a turkey! We forgot to get it yesterday, didn't we? What are we going to do?'

'Tut, tut,' said Maddie, shaking her head. 'You'll have to go out for dinner somewhere.'

Jake looked at me, clearly stricken. I could see him silently pleading with me not to take him to Maddie's. Christmas dinner with Wayne would be one step too far, even if he had Baxter to console him.

'I do know somewhere we can go for dinner,' I said thoughtfully. 'It's a lovely little place, and the owner is probably cooking as we speak. Hmm. I suppose we could go there.'

'I'll give you a lift if you like,' Maddie offered, her eyes twinkling.

I nodded. 'That would be wonderful. Thank you. Get your coat and shoes on, Jake.' He stood up, his expression revealing his anxiety. 'But what about Baxter? We can't leave him here on his own.'

'Quite right,' Maddie said.

'Don't worry,' I reassured him. 'Baxter can come with us. I'm sure he'd appreciate a Christmas dinner too.'

'Really?' Jake's eyes lit up and he ran to get his shoes and coat, with Baxter bounding behind him.

'Thanks for this, Maddie,' I whispered, and she hugged me.

'No problem at all. I'm just so happy that everything's worked out for you both — and for Baxter. It's such a relief, I can't tell you.'

'And the couple didn't mind?'

'I think they were having second thoughts anyway. When I went round to break the news they were looking at a reference book about West Highland Whites. They tried to hide it under the cushion pretty sharpish though.'

Jake returned, and I grabbed my own coat and took hold of Baxter's lead.

'Right then,' I said. 'Let's go.'

***

Glamis Avenue looked like a scene from a cosy Christmas film, with the red roofs and neat hedges of its pretty little bungalows laced in the snow that was coming down in soft flakes.

As Maddie pulled up outside number twenty-seven, Jake looked around in surprise. 'This isn't a restaurant,' he said. 'Where are we?'

Maddie leaned over and planted a kiss on his cheek. 'Merry Christmas, Jakey,' she said, her eyes glittering with tears. 'You have a brilliant day and look after Baxter for me.'

'What do you mean? Is he staying with me? Really?'

'Let's just say he's not my dog any more,' she confirmed, smiling. She glanced up at me, as I stood beside the car, my stomach churning with nerves.

'Ring me tomorrow,' she whispered, and I nodded, helping Jake out onto the grass verge, and taking a tight hold of Baxter's lead.

She waved and drove off, leaving us standing in front of the little wrought iron gate. 'Mum, what are we doing here?' Jake asked, his little face pinched with worry. 'Who lives here? I thought we were having Christmas dinner?'

'We are, Jakey,' I said, ruffling his hair. 'We've been invited over by someone very special. Look.'

He turned his head, and as Dylan opened the front door and stood there smiling at us, his eyes widened. I pushed open the gate and had to forcibly restrain Baxter from hurling himself down the path as Jake ran towards the door. I didn't want Baxter to send him flying, snow or no snow.

With a lump in my throat I watched as Dylan opened his arms and Jake flew into them.

'Merry Christmas, Jakey,' Dylan said, picking him up and hugging him. 'And I see you've brought Baxter with you. I hope you're hungry. I've cooked enough to feed an army.'

He looked at me as I crunched up to them, still battling to keep Baxter in check. His free arm wrapped around me, and he pulled me into an embrace. We stood, the four of us together, as the snowflakes drifted down around us. I could have stayed like that forever, but Baxter had other ideas, and Dylan laughed and stepped aside to let him bound indoors and reclaim his home.

***

'I don't think I could eat another thing.' I heaved a huge sigh and leaned back in my chair. 'You can really cook.'

'Why, thank you,' Dylan said. 'And what do you think, Jakey? Did you enjoy it?'

'It was scrummy,' Jake confirmed. He looked from Dylan to me, his blue eyes shining. 'So, now we've had dinner, are you going to give me my present?'

Dylan and I exchanged glances, and Dylan winked at me. 'Well, I don't know about that. I mean, we haven't had our Christmas pudding yet have we? And we ought to have another drink, to toast the season. Don't you agree, Ellie?'

'Oh, definitely,' I said, nodding furiously.

Jake looked appalled. 'But you've just said you couldn't eat another thing! I don't like Christmas pudding, and surely you can wait for a while? Anyway,' he added wisely, 'you shouldn't eat so much in one sitting. You'll get indigestion.'

'He's got a point,' said Dylan. 'So, Ellie, do you think we should give him his present now?'

'Hmm.' I considered the matter. 'Maybe I should load the dishwasher first, what do you think?'

'Oh, no.' Dylan shook his head. 'You've gone too far there. Today I'm going to take care of you. You're not going to lift a finger.'

'Wow,' I gasped. 'You really are the perfect man, aren't you?'

He laughed. 'I doubt Greg and Colleen would agree. Though how was I to know that Lucy would decorate their lounge wall with such gusto — I thought buying her paints for Christmas would just encourage her artistic talents. It's hardly my fault she didn't use paper.'

'Never mind all that,' said Jake impatiently. 'Dylan, you said that you had a present for me and I could have it as soon as we had dinner. We've finished dinner now, so what is it?'

I looked at Dylan, who nodded. We stood up and Dylan took Jake's hand, leading him into the hallway and nodding at two open doors.

'So, which room do you reckon, Jakey?'

Jake frowned. 'What do you mean, which room? You mean, my present's in one of them? Do I have to guess?'

Dylan shook his head. 'No. I mean, which of those two rooms would you prefer for your bedroom?'

Jake gaped at him. 'My bedroom? You mean…?' He looked at me, then back at Dylan again. 'Are we going to live here, in your bungalow? Really? With you?'

Dylan looked at him anxiously. 'Is that all right with you? Would you mind living here?'

'Mind? Are you crackers?'

I don't think Jake could have smiled any wider if he'd tried.

'And I can choose my own room? Really?'

We nodded, and he threw his arms around Baxter's neck. 'Did you hear that, boy? We're going to be living here, forever and ever.' He looked up at us both, suddenly concerned. 'Baxter can live here too, can't he?'

'Most definitely,' Dylan said.

'And it *will* be forever and ever, won't it?'

'You don't have to worry about that,' Dylan reassured him. 'This is your home now. Yours, Baxter's, and your mum's. And as far as I'm concerned, yes, it's forever and ever.'

I blinked back tears as my son dashed between the two rooms, Baxter following closely behind him.

Jake checked out the view from each window while considering the matter carefully. 'I think this one. It's bigger, and that means Baxter can sleep in here too,' he said eventually.

'This one it is then. We'll have a trip to the DIY shop tomorrow shall we? You can pick out some wallpaper. In fact,' Dylan added with a laugh, 'you can choose some new furniture too. The Boxing Day sales will be on, so we'll push the boat out. I wonder if they do a Thunderbirds design wallpaper?'

'Really? Brilliant!' Jake planted a kiss on Baxter's nose. 'You see, Baxter? This is the best Christmas ever. Mum and Dylan are getting married, and you'll never have to miss us again.'

As my face started to burn, I held up my hands in protest. 'Er, no, Jakey, we didn't say—'

Dylan spun me round, planting a kiss on my lips before I could finish the sentence. 'And we didn't *not* say it either,' he whispered. 'He only mentioned it before I got the chance, that's all.'

'Are you serious? Don't you think this is moving a bit fast?' I said, trying to be sensible while ignoring the surge of delight bubbling up inside me.

'Personally, I think I've waited long enough to find this kind of happiness,' he said. 'But don't listen to me. What does your little voice say?'

I paused then smiled. 'It's telling me to snap you up before someone else does.'

'Always trust that little voice,' he said and kissed me again. Behind us, Jake was telling Baxter about all the things they were going to do, since no one was ever going to separate them again.

'And we can play in the garden, and I can take you to the park every day, and you can come to the wedding, and you'll have to wear a tie. And then, after Mum and Dylan get married, I'll get a new baby brother or sister, and you can help me look after them.'

My mouth dropped open and I turned to Dylan, expecting to see a look of horror on his face, but he just grinned at me. 'Sounds like a plan.'

'It does?' I shook my head, amazed. 'What happened to the man who never wanted marriage, never wanted children?'

'He's long gone,' said Dylan, nuzzling my neck and giving a contented sigh. 'And it's all because of you.'

'Oh no it's not, Dylan,' called Jake, laughing as the Boxer chased him out of his new bedroom and along the hallway, barking joyfully. 'It's all because of Baxter!'

'He's got a point there,' I said. 'If it hadn't been for Baxter…'

I shuddered. Dylan wrapped me in his arms and held me, and I knew I didn't need words to explain what I was feeling.

The three of us had been waifs and strays, and this Christmas had promised to be the bleakest one of all.

But a miracle had happened.

We had Dylan. We had each other. We were home.

Sign up for Sharon's newsletter at
www.sharonboothwriter.com/newsletter-sign-up
and get all her latest news, cover reveals, release dates
and more, including the chance to win a prize every
month.

Also in the Home for Christmas series

The Other Side of Christmas

A festive feel-good novella. Katy's driving home for Christmas – except an empty, cold caravan hardly seems like home, and it's not feeling much like Christmas.

It wasn't supposed to be like this: a few months ago she had her dream cottage, a loving fiance, and big plans for a perfect wedding. Now she's in her car, travelling through the snow along dark, country lanes, heading towards a Christmas spent by herself, with nothing more to look forward to than a frozen turkey dinner and a box of Quality Street.

With her friends busy with their guests, her parents on a cruise, and her ex-fiance miles away, the only person Katy is expecting to see at all is Luke, the builder who has been working hard to transform Katy's cottage before it goes up for sale on the other side of Christmas.

Arriving at last in the Holderness village of Weltringham, she's disappointed to find both the cottage and the caravan in darkness, and Luke nowhere to be seen. It seems everyone in the world has abandoned her to her gloomy fate.

Is she doomed to have the worst festive season ever, or is someone about to save Katy's Christmas?

Take a break from those Christmas preparations and curl up by the fire for a couple of hours with this seasonal cosy read

Christmas with Cary

You never forget your first love.

Molly's spent every Christmas she can remember surrounded by her family. But this year is different. This year, Molly's all alone in a strange town. She's left her family behind, and she's not sure where she can call home any longer. All Molly has with her are a few clothes in a suitcase, and a collection of her old friend's Cary Grant films.

Except, there's one more thing she's brought along - the whole reason for her Christmas visit. In her possession is a small, crumpled piece of paper, and on it is written the address of the love of her life.

Molly and Cary have had many chances over the years, but somehow life kept getting in the way and they always ended up apart once more. Yet Molly has never forgotten the first man she gave her heart to, and now she has one last chance to win him back.

But will Cary welcome her home, or will he tell her what she dreads to hear - that they've had their chance, and it's all too late. That's if she can even find him...

A cosy, festive story about hope, forgiveness, and never giving up on love - however long it takes.

Printed in Great Britain
by Amazon